JURASSIC PARK™

VOLUME 6

DARK CARGO!

ADAPTED BY
STEVE ENGLEHART,
ARMANDO GIL
AND DELL BARRAS

Spotlight

IDW™

visit us at www.abdopublishing.com

Reinforced library bound editions published in 2014 by Spotlight, a division of the ABDO Group, PO Box 398166, Minneapolis, Minnesota 55439. Published by agreement with IDW Publishing. www.idwpublishing.com

Printed in the United States of America, North Mankato, Minnesota.
052013
092013
♻ This book contains at least 10% recycled materials.

Library of Congress Cataloging-in-Publication Data

Englehart, Steve.
  Jurassic Park / adapted by Steve Englehart, Armand Gil, and Dell Barras. -- Reinforced library edition.
       pages cm. -- (Jurassic Park ; v. 5-10)
  Summary: "Three days after their escape from Isla Nublar, Dr. Alan Grant and Dr. Ellie Sattler have returned to help confine the dinosaurs. When the escaped raptors remain elusive, Grant and Sattler go on their own mission... and discover they aren't the only ones looking for raptors!"-- Provided by publisher.
  ISBN 978-1-61479-187-4 (vol. 5: Aftershocks!) -- ISBN 978-1-61479-188-1 (vol. 6: Dark cargo!) -- ISBN 978-1-61479-189-8 (vol. 7: Raptors attack) -- ISBN 978-1-61479-190-4 (vol. 8: Animals vs. men) -- ISBN 978-1-61479-191-1 (vol. 9: Animals vs. gods!) -- ISBN 978-1-61479-192-8 (vol. 10: Gods vs. men!)
  1. Graphic novels. [1. Graphic novels. 2. Dinosaurs--Fiction. 3. Science fiction.] I. Gil, Armand. II. Barras, Dell. III. Title.
  PZ7.7.E6Jur 2013
  741.5'973--dc23
                                          2013013372

All Spotlight books are reinforced library binding and manufactured in the United States of America.

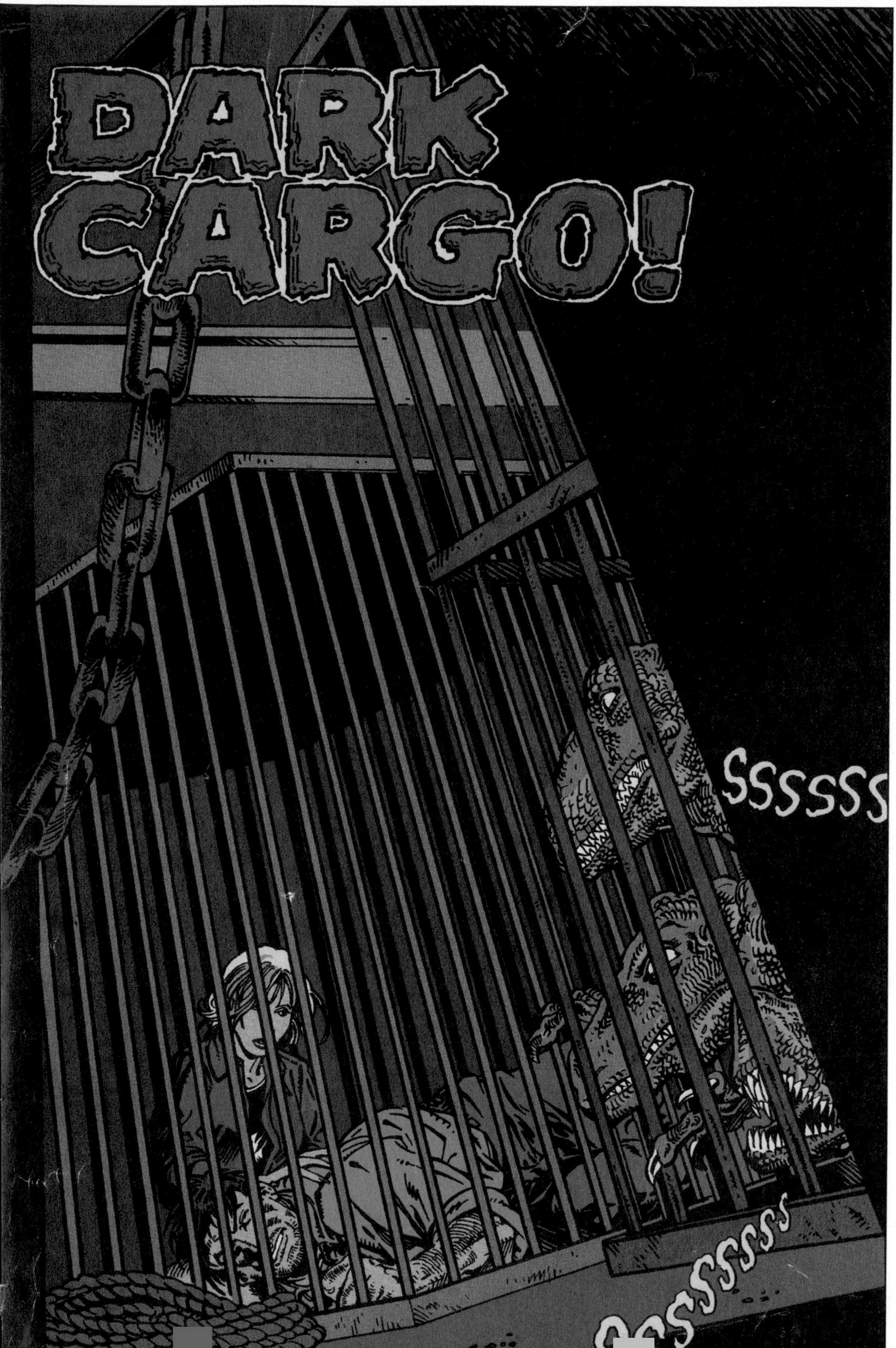
DARK CARGO!
SSSSSS
SSSSSSSSSSS

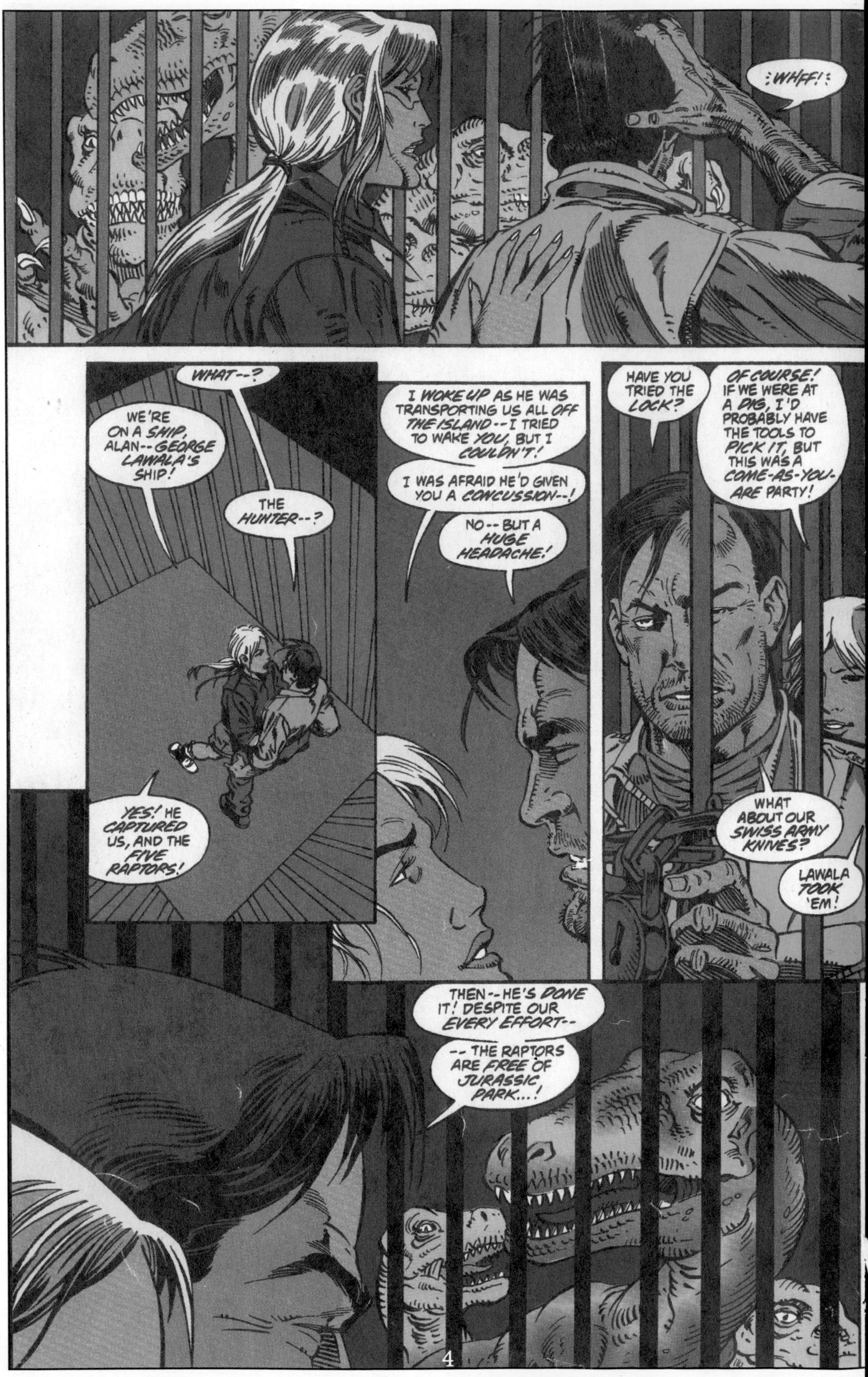
:WHFF!:
WHAT--?
WE'RE ON A SHIP, ALAN--GEORGE LAWALA'S SHIP!
THE HUNTER--?
YES! HE CAPTURED US, AND THE FIVE RAPTORS!
I WOKE UP AS HE WAS TRANSPORTING US ALL OFF THE ISLAND--I TRIED TO WAKE YOU, BUT I COULDN'T!
I WAS AFRAID HE'D GIVEN YOU A CONCUSSION--!
NO--BUT A HUGE HEADACHE!
HAVE YOU TRIED THE LOCK?
OF COURSE! IF WE WERE AT A DIG, I'D PROBABLY HAVE THE TOOLS TO PICK IT, BUT THIS WAS A COME-AS-YOU-ARE PARTY!
WHAT ABOUT OUR SWISS ARMY KNIVES?
LAWALA TOOK 'EM!
THEN--HE'S DONE IT! DESPITE OUR EVERY EFFORT--
--THE RAPTORS ARE FREE OF JURASSIC PARK...!

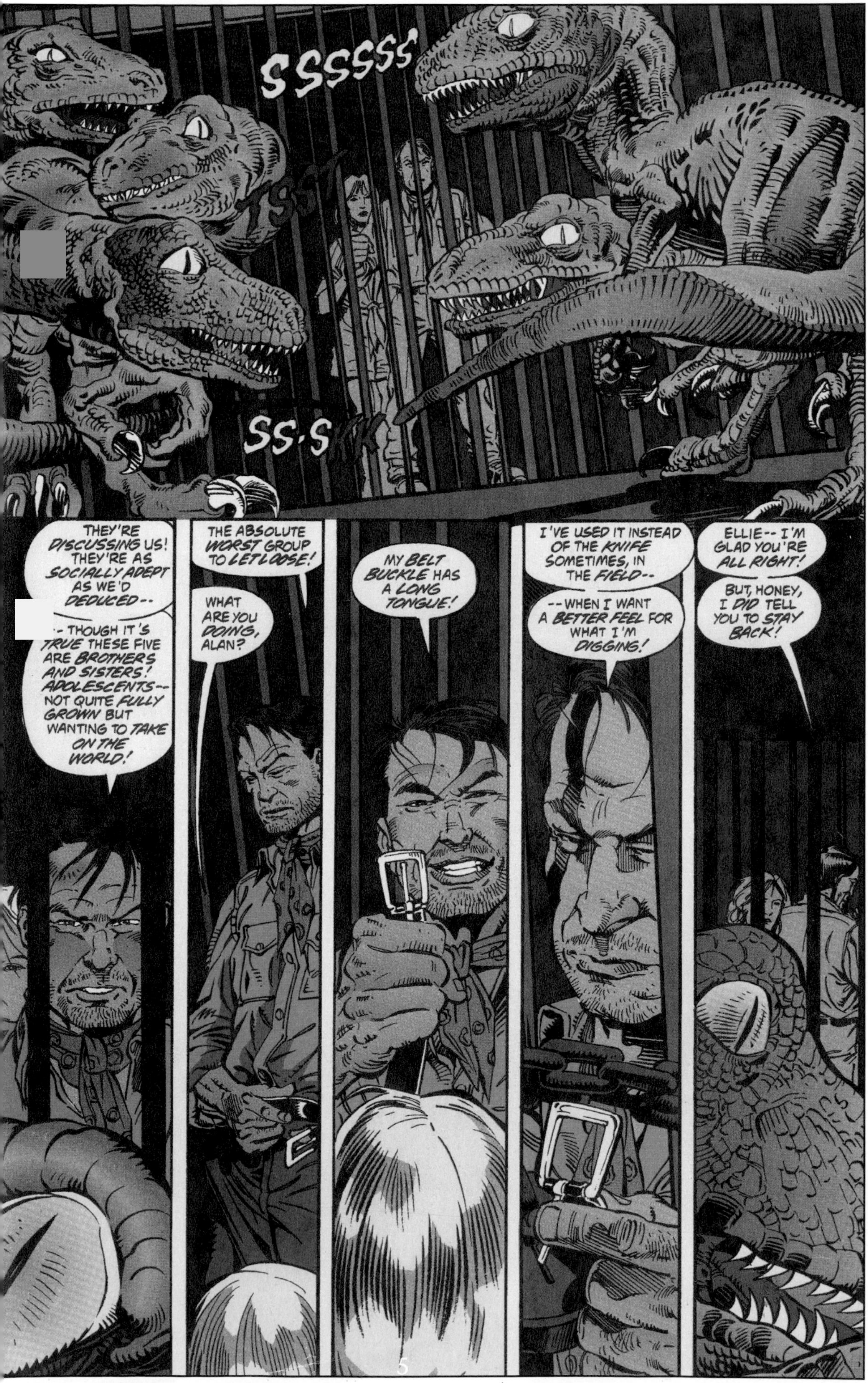
SSSSSS
THEY'RE DISCUSSING US! THEY'RE AS SOCIALLY ADEPT AS WE'D DEDUCED--
-- THOUGH IT'S TRUE THESE FIVE ARE BROTHERS AND SISTERS! ADOLESCENTS-- NOT QUITE FULLY GROWN BUT WANTING TO TAKE ON THE WORLD!
THE ABSOLUTE WORST GROUP TO LET LOOSE!
WHAT ARE YOU DOING, ALAN?
MY BELT BUCKLE HAS A LONG TONGUE!
I'VE USED IT INSTEAD OF THE KNIFE SOMETIMES, IN THE FIELD--
--WHEN I WANT A BETTER FEEL FOR WHAT I'M DIGGING!
ELLIE-- I'M GLAD YOU'RE ALL RIGHT!
BUT, HONEY, I DID TELL YOU TO STAY BACK!

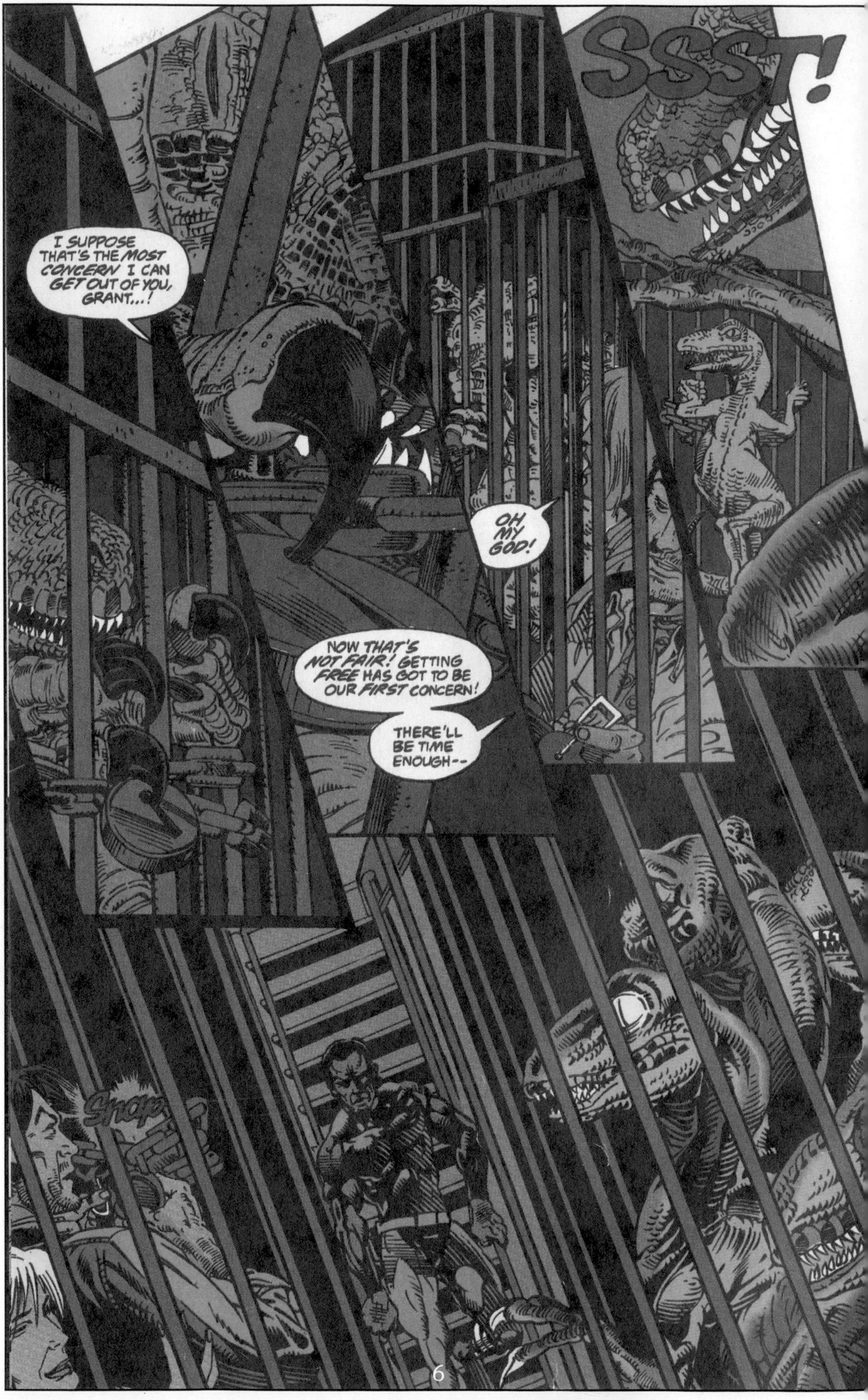
SSST!
I SUPPOSE THAT'S THE MOST CONCERN I CAN GET OUT OF YOU, GRANT...!
OH MY GOD!
NOW THAT'S NOT FAIR! GETTING FREE HAS GOT TO BE OUR FIRST CONCERN!
THERE'LL BE TIME ENOUGH--
Snap

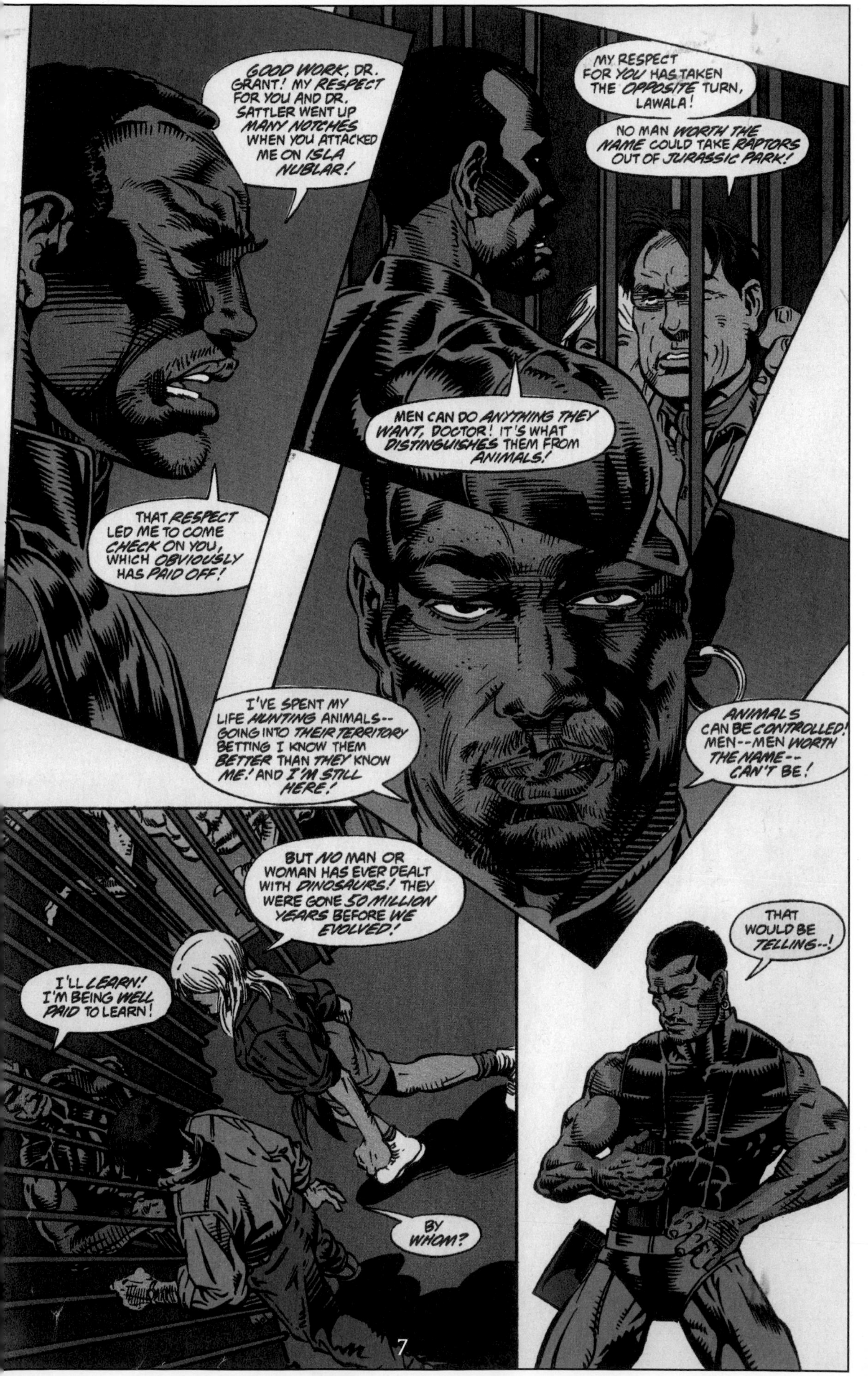
GOOD WORK, DR. GRANT! MY RESPECT FOR YOU AND DR. SATTLER WENT UP MANY NOTCHES WHEN YOU ATTACKED ME ON ISLA NUBLAR!
MY RESPECT FOR YOU HAS TAKEN THE OPPOSITE TURN, LAWALA!
NO MAN WORTH THE NAME COULD TAKE RAPTORS OUT OF JURASSIC PARK!
THAT RESPECT LED ME TO COME CHECK ON YOU, WHICH OBVIOUSLY HAS PAID OFF!
MEN CAN DO ANYTHING THEY WANT, DOCTOR! IT'S WHAT DISTINGUISHES THEM FROM ANIMALS!
I'VE SPENT MY LIFE HUNTING ANIMALS-- GOING INTO THEIR TERRITORY BETTING I KNOW THEM BETTER THAN THEY KNOW ME! AND I'M STILL HERE!
ANIMALS CAN BE CONTROLLED! MEN--MEN WORTH THE NAME-- CAN'T BE!
BUT NO MAN OR WOMAN HAS EVER DEALT WITH DINOSAURS! THEY WERE GONE 50 MILLION YEARS BEFORE WE EVOLVED!
I'LL LEARN! I'M BEING WELL PAID TO LEARN!
BY WHOM?
THAT WOULD BE TELLING--!

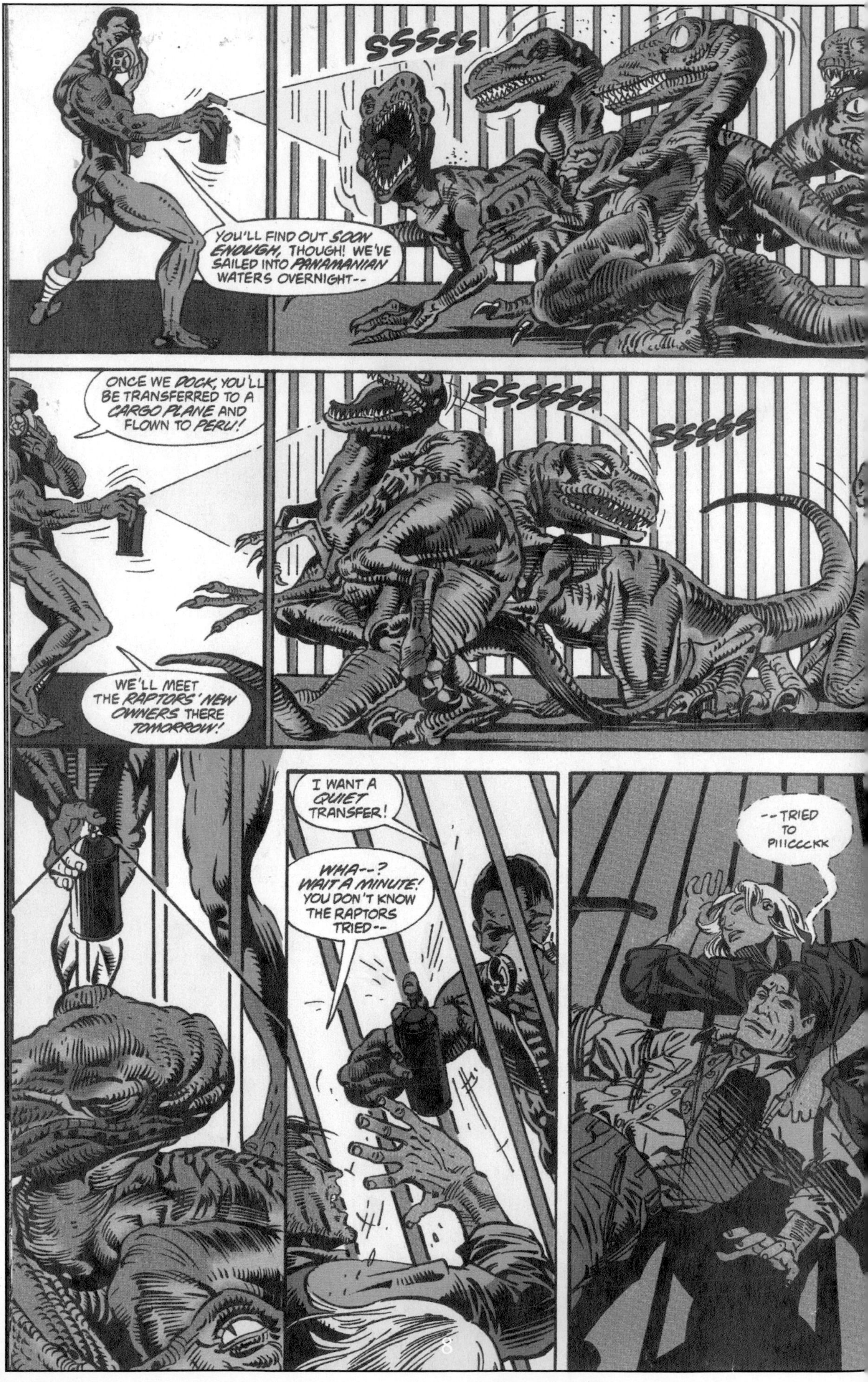
SSSSS
YOU'LL FIND OUT SOON ENOUGH, THOUGH! WE'VE SAILED INTO PANAMANIAN WATERS OVERNIGHT--
ONCE WE DOCK, YOU'LL BE TRANSFERRED TO A CARGO PLANE AND FLOWN TO PERU!
SSSSSS
SSSSS
WE'LL MEET THE RAPTORS' NEW OWNERS THERE TOMORROW!
I WANT A QUIET TRANSFER!
WHA--? WAIT A MINUTE! YOU DON'T KNOW THE RAPTORS TRIED--
--TRIED TO PIIICCCKK

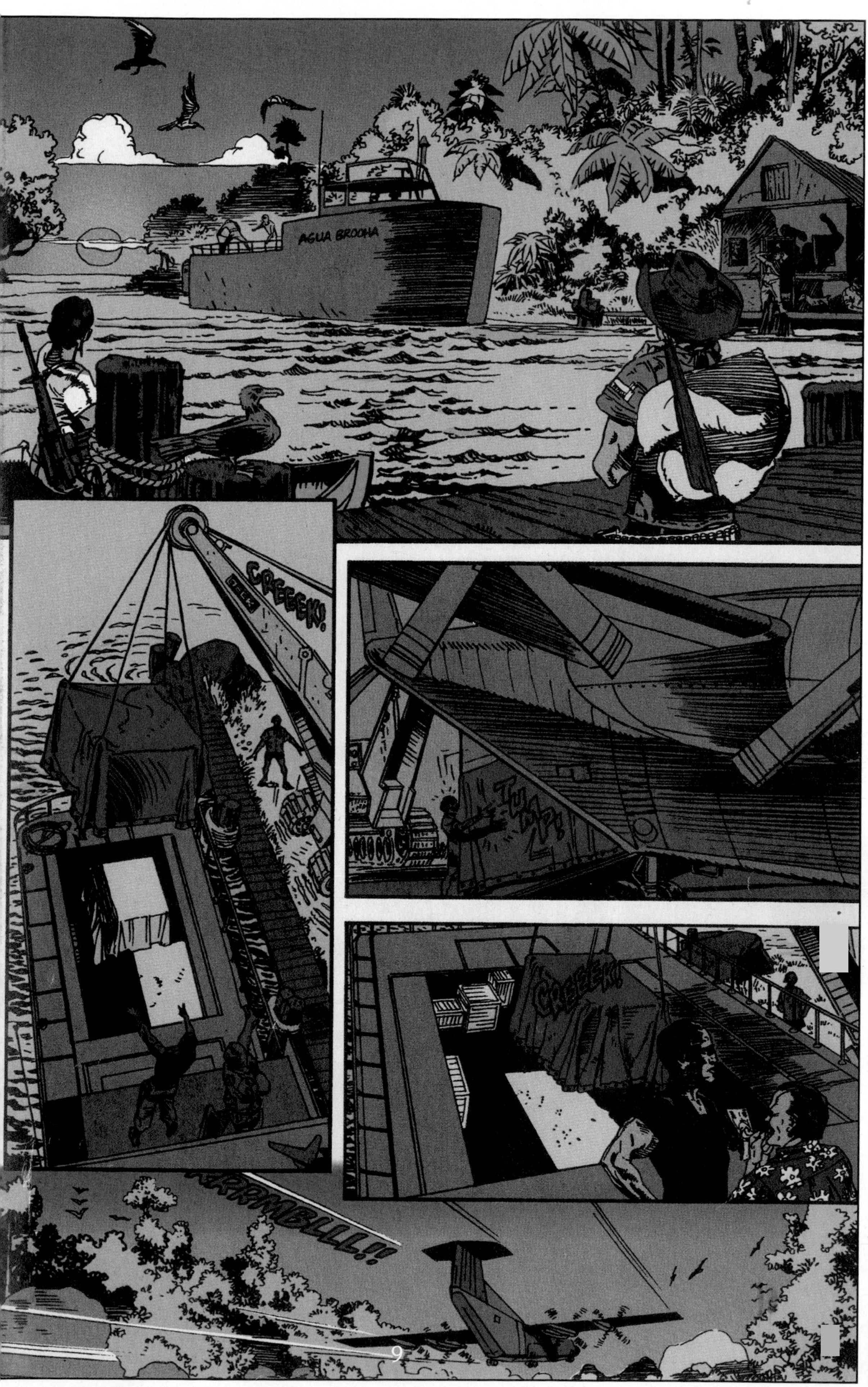
AGUA BROOHA
CREEEK!
THUMP!
CREEEK!
RRRMBLLLL!!

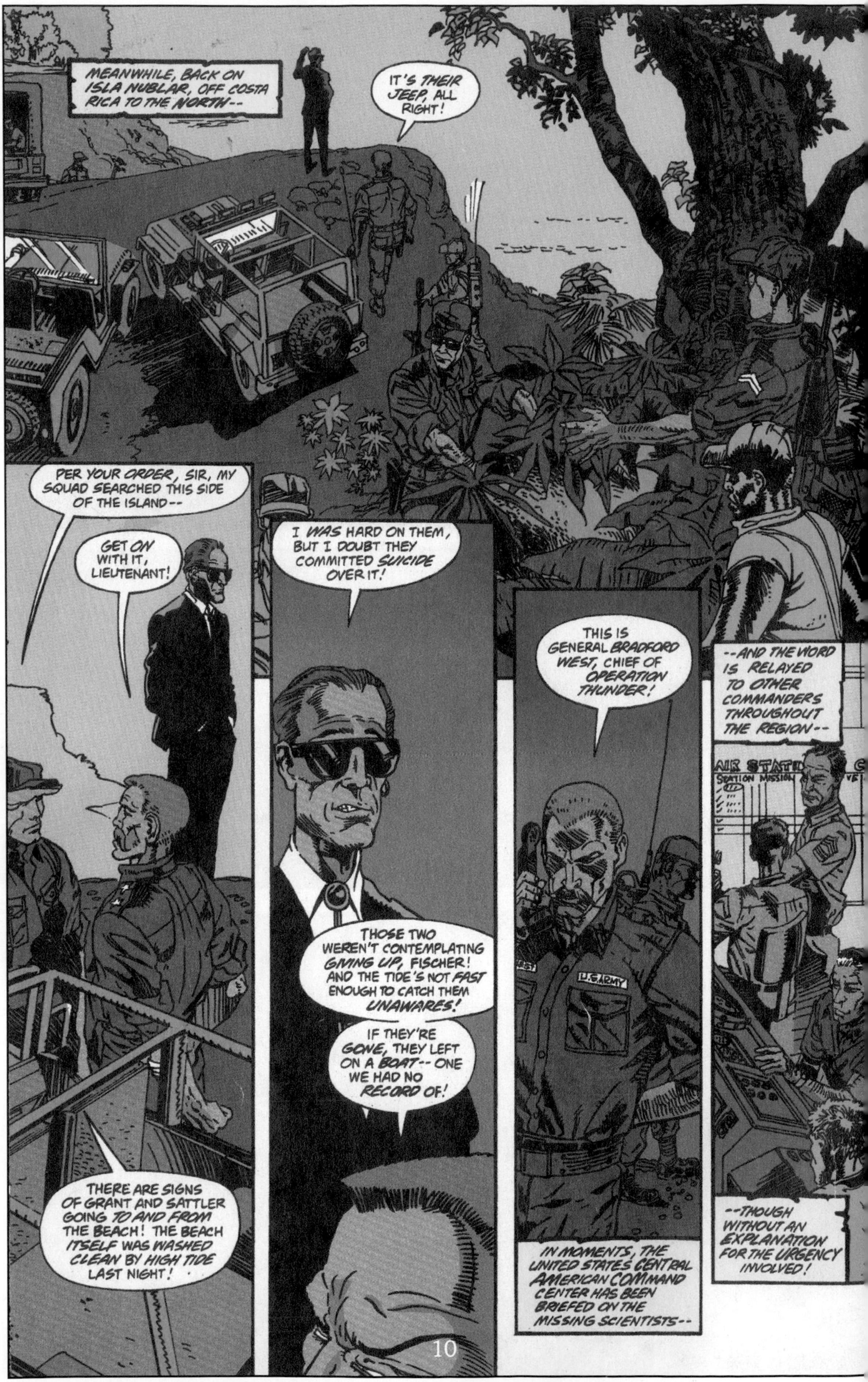

MEANWHILE, BACK ON ISLA NUBLAR, OFF COSTA RICA TO THE NORTH--
IT'S THEIR JEEP, ALL RIGHT!
PER YOUR ORDER, SIR, MY SQUAD SEARCHED THIS SIDE OF THE ISLAND--
GET ON WITH IT, LIEUTENANT!
THERE ARE SIGNS OF GRANT AND SATTLER GOING TO AND FROM THE BEACH! THE BEACH ITSELF WAS WASHED CLEAN BY HIGH TIDE LAST NIGHT!
I WAS HARD ON THEM, BUT I DOUBT THEY COMMITTED SUICIDE OVER IT!
THOSE TWO WEREN'T CONTEMPLATING GIVING UP, FISCHER! AND THE TIDE'S NOT FAST ENOUGH TO CATCH THEM UNAWARES!
IF THEY'RE GONE, THEY LEFT ON A BOAT-- ONE WE HAD NO RECORD OF!
THIS IS GENERAL BRADFORD WEST, CHIEF OF OPERATION THUNDER!
U.S. ARMY
IN MOMENTS, THE UNITED STATES CENTRAL AMERICAN COMMAND CENTER HAS BEEN BRIEFED ON THE MISSING SCIENTISTS--
--AND THE WORD IS RELAYED TO OTHER COMMANDERS THROUGHOUT THE REGION--
--THOUGH WITHOUT AN EXPLANATION FOR THE URGENCY INVOLVED!

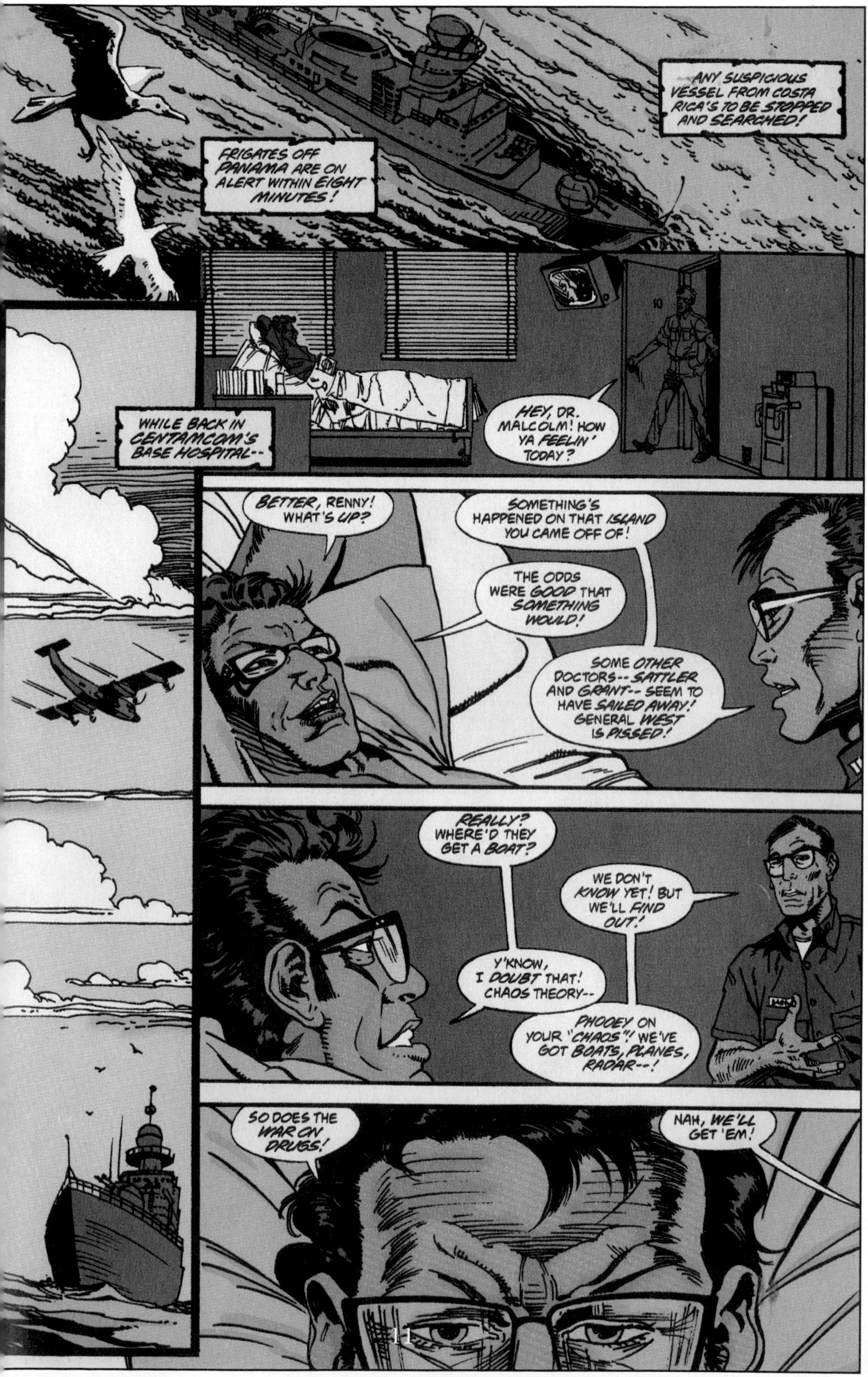
FRIGATES OFF PANAMA ARE ON ALERT WITHIN EIGHT MINUTES!
ANY SUSPICIOUS VESSEL FROM COSTA RICA'S TO BE STOPPED AND SEARCHED!
WHILE BACK IN CENTAMCOM'S BASE HOSPITAL--
HEY, DR. MALCOLM! HOW YA FEELIN' TODAY?
BETTER, RENNY! WHAT'S UP?
SOMETHING'S HAPPENED ON THAT ISLAND YOU CAME OFF OF!
THE ODDS WERE GOOD THAT SOMETHING WOULD!
SOME OTHER DOCTORS-- SATTLER AND GRANT-- SEEM TO HAVE SAILED AWAY! GENERAL WEST IS PISSED!
REALLY? WHERE'D THEY GET A BOAT?
WE DON'T KNOW YET! BUT WE'LL FIND OUT!
Y'KNOW, I DOUBT THAT! CHAOS THEORY--
PHOOEY ON YOUR "CHAOS"! WE'VE GOT BOATS, PLANES, RADAR--!
SO DOES THE WAR ON DRUGS!
NAH, WE'LL GET 'EM!

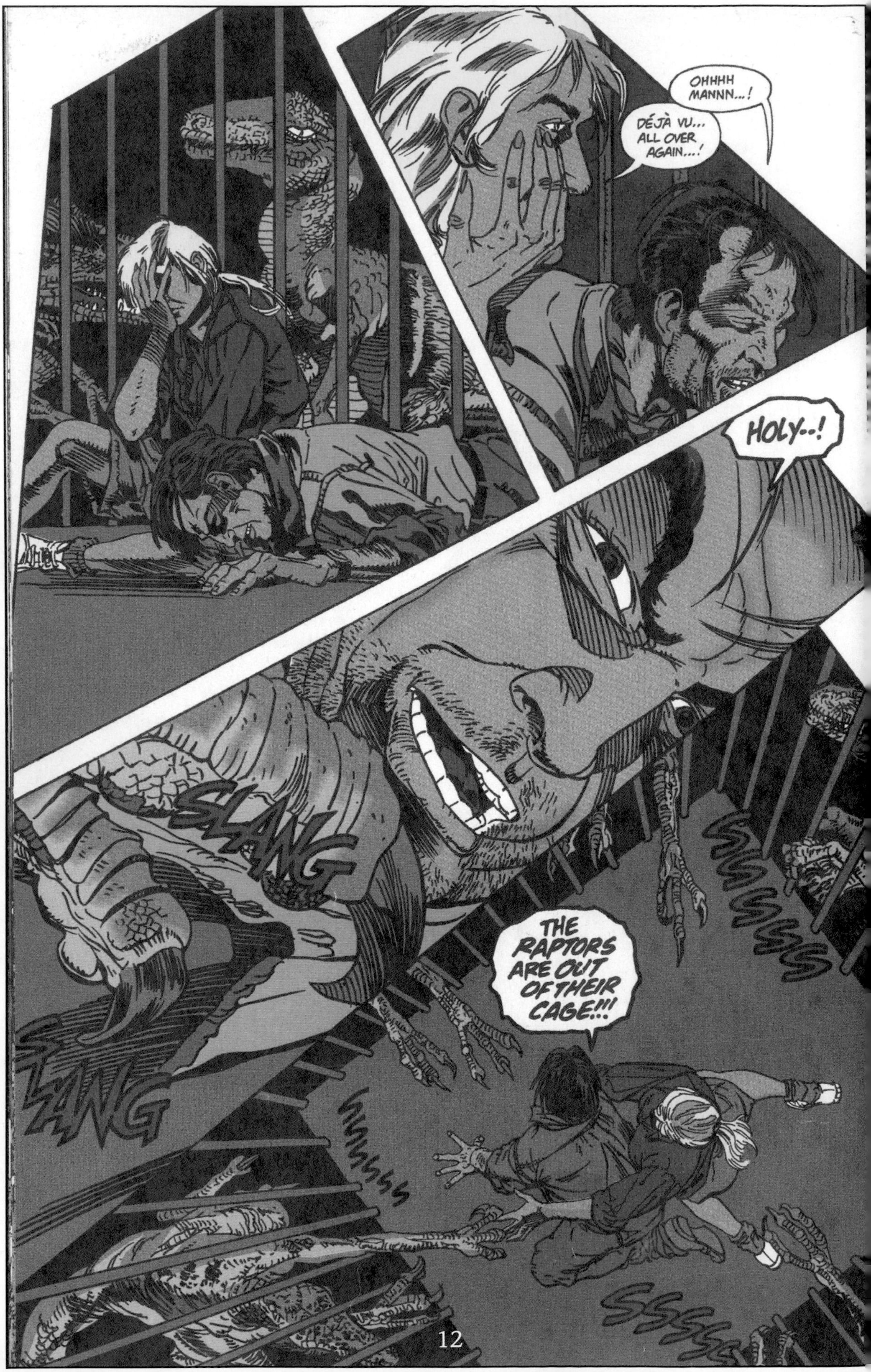
OHHHH MANNN...!
DÉJÀ VU... ALL OVER AGAIN...!
HOLY--!
SLANG
SSSSSS
THE RAPTORS ARE OUT OF THEIR CAGE!!!
SLANG
SSSSS

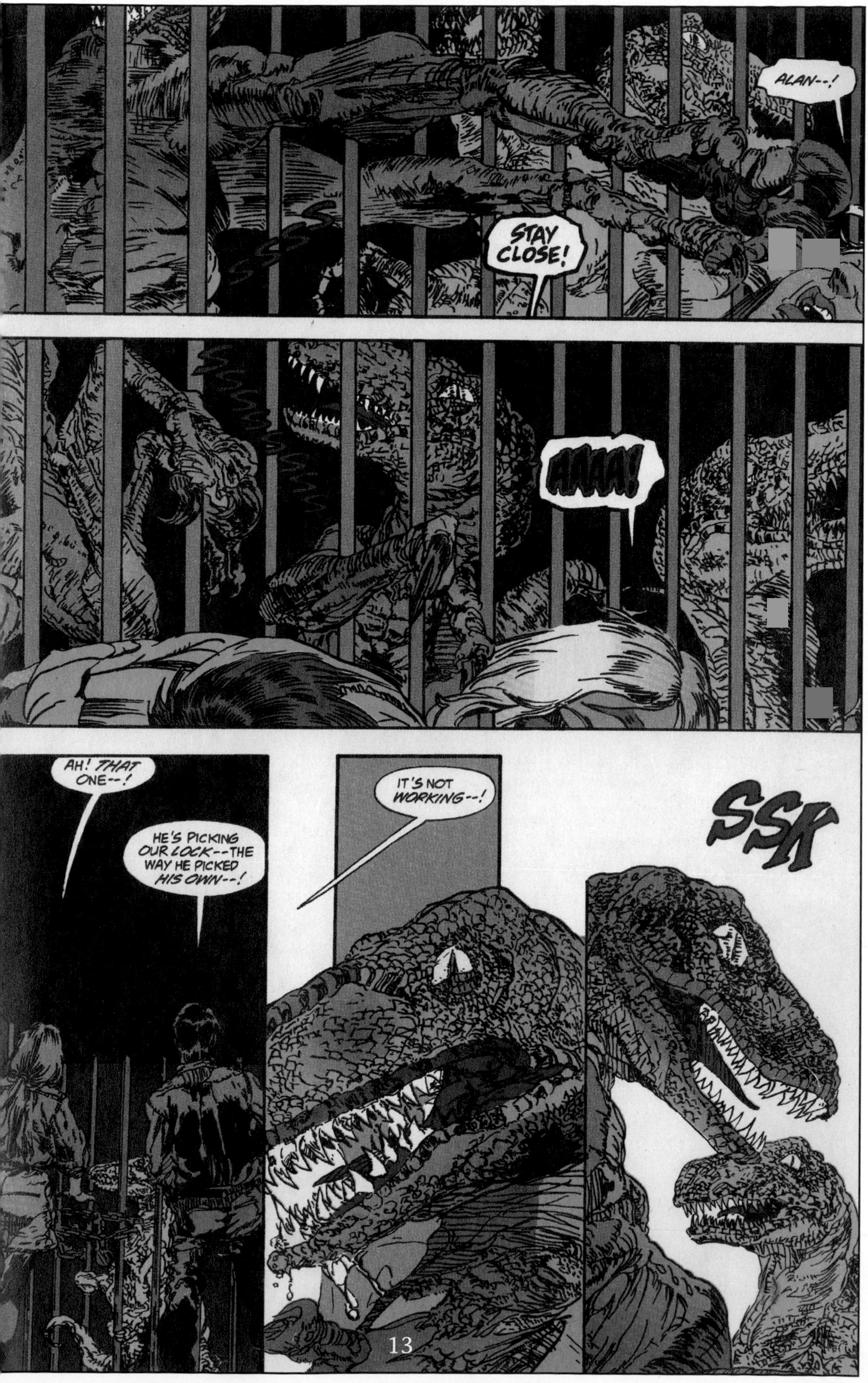
ALAN--!
STAY CLOSE!
AAAA!
AH! THAT ONE--!
HE'S PICKING OUR LOCK--THE WAY HE PICKED HIS OWN--!
IT'S NOT WORKING--!
SSK

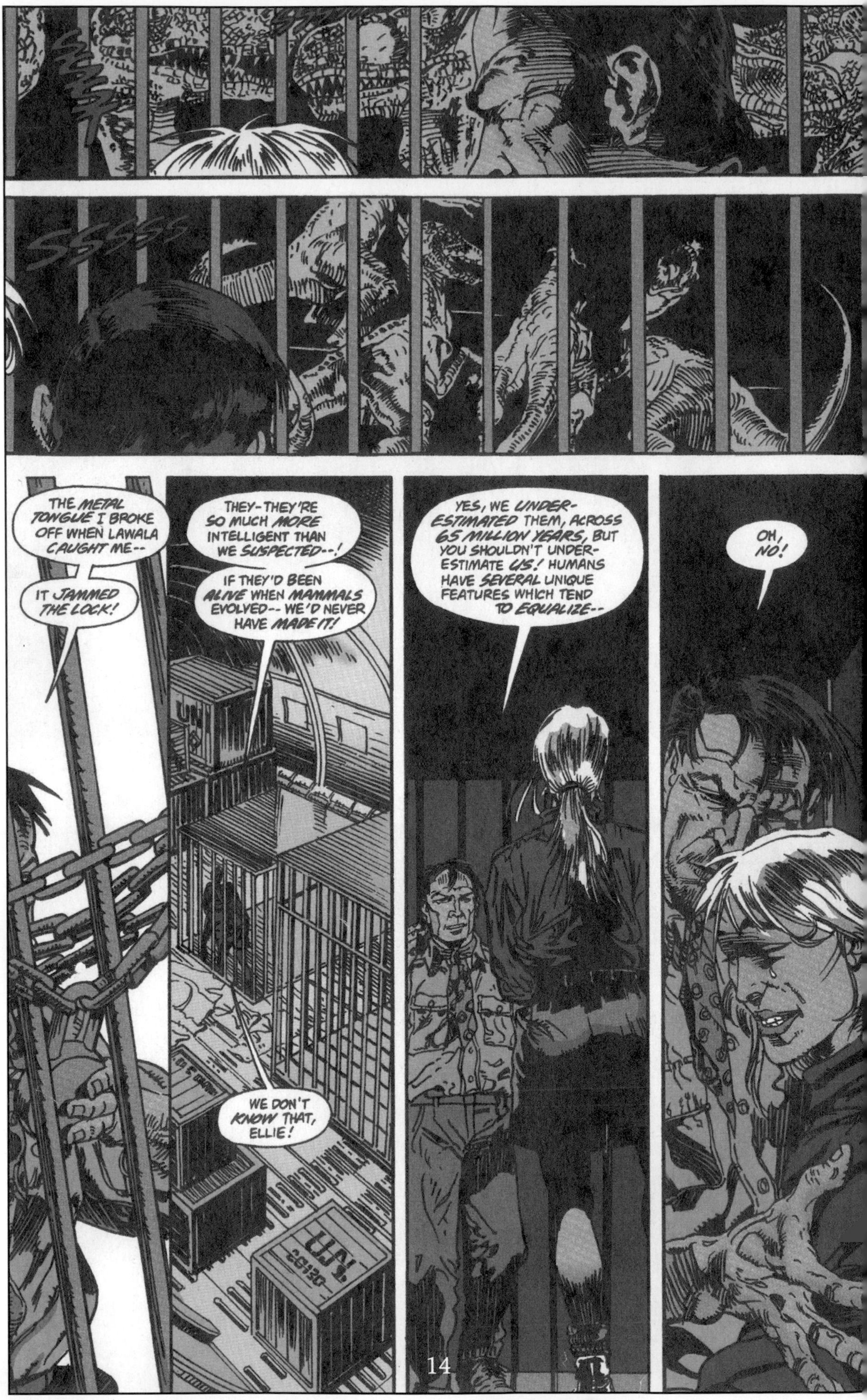
SNAP
SSSSSS
THE METAL TONGUE I BROKE OFF WHEN LAWALA CAUGHT ME--
IT JAMMED THE LOCK!
THEY-THEY'RE SO MUCH MORE INTELLIGENT THAN WE SUSPECTED--!
IF THEY'D BEEN ALIVE WHEN MAMMALS EVOLVED-- WE'D NEVER HAVE MADE IT!
WE DON'T KNOW THAT, ELLIE!
YES, WE UNDER-ESTIMATED THEM, ACROSS 65 MILLION YEARS, BUT YOU SHOULDN'T UNDER-ESTIMATE US! HUMANS HAVE SEVERAL UNIQUE FEATURES WHICH TEND TO EQUALIZE--
OH, NO!

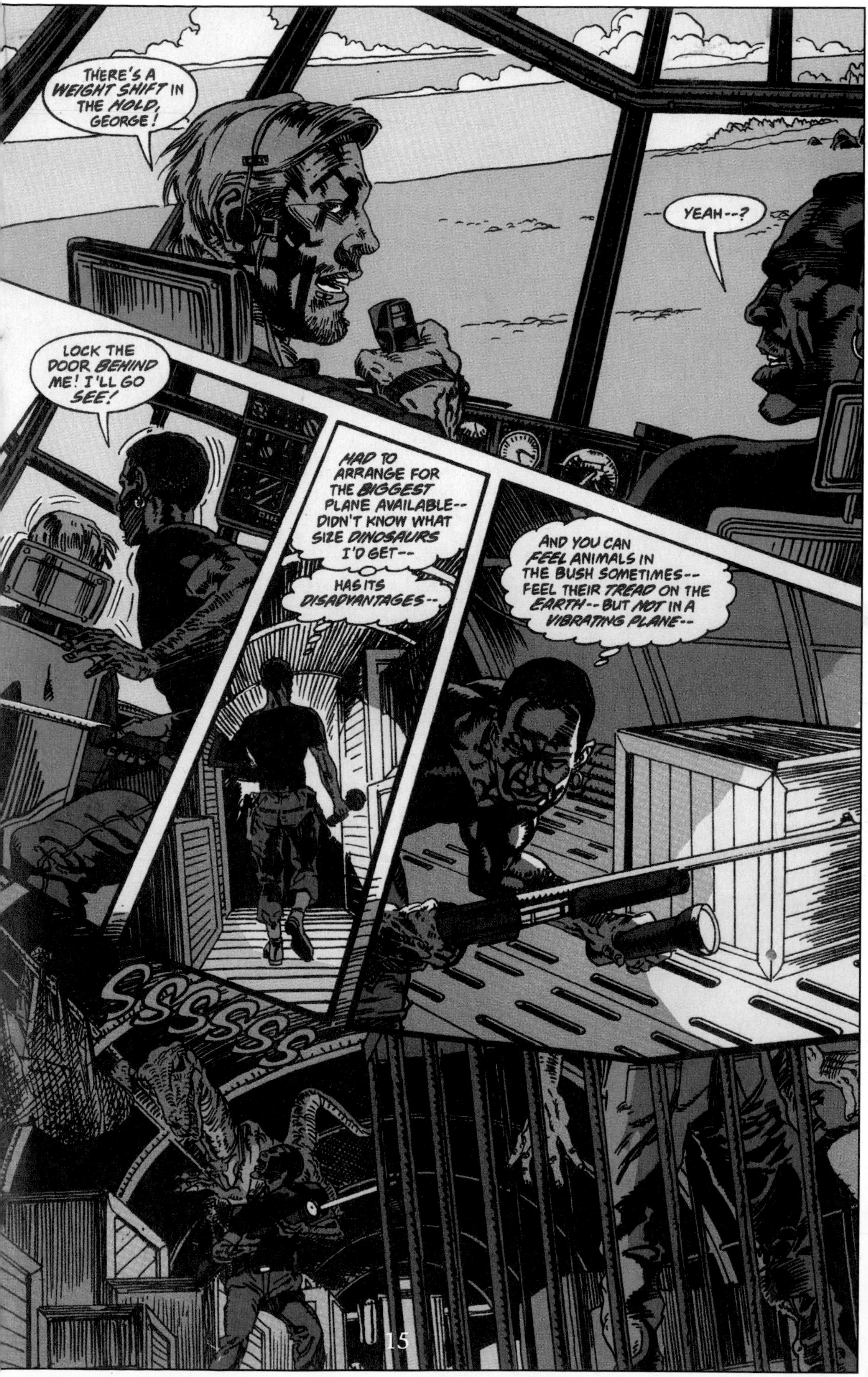
THERE'S A WEIGHT SHIFT IN THE HOLD, GEORGE!
YEAH--?
LOCK THE DOOR BEHIND ME! I'LL GO SEE!
HAD TO ARRANGE FOR THE BIGGEST PLANE AVAILABLE-- DIDN'T KNOW WHAT SIZE DINOSAURS I'D GET--
HAS ITS DISADVANTAGES--
AND YOU CAN FEEL ANIMALS IN THE BUSH SOMETIMES-- FEEL THEIR TREAD ON THE EARTH--BUT NOT IN A VIBRATING PLANE--
SSSSSS

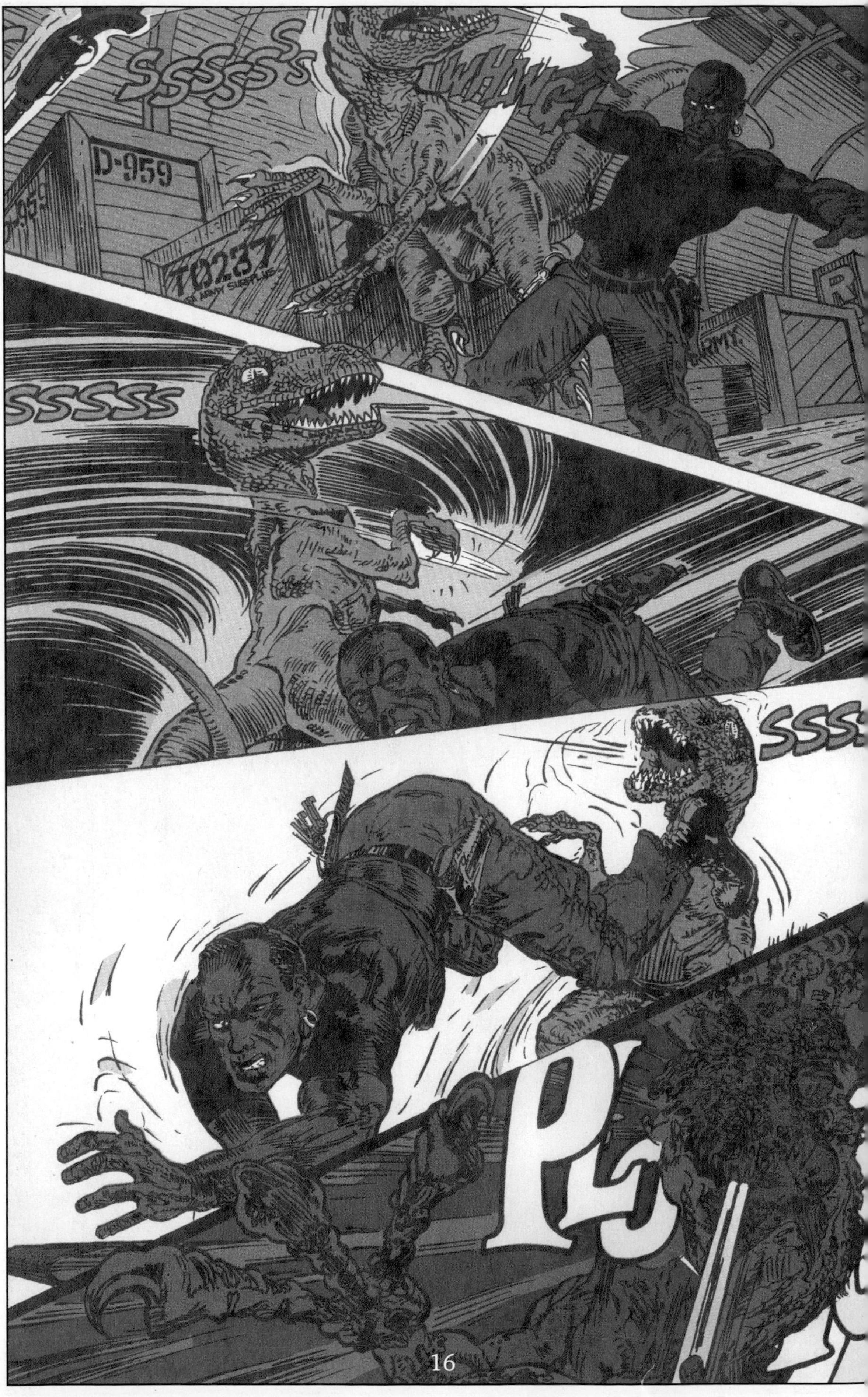
SSSSSSSS
WHANG!
D-959
D-959
T0237
SSSSSS
SSSS
PL

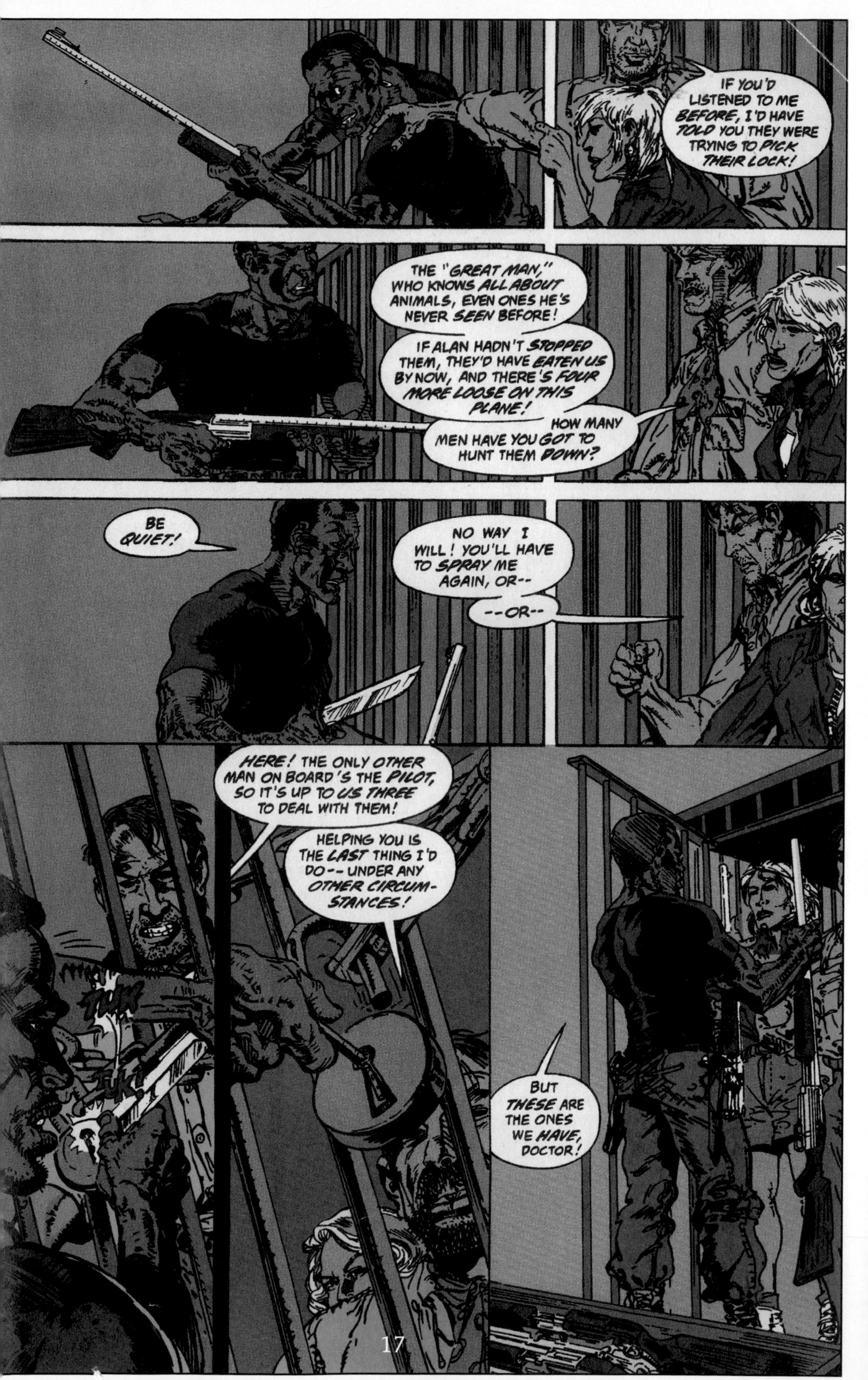
IF YOU'D LISTENED TO ME BEFORE, I'D HAVE TOLD YOU THEY WERE TRYING TO PICK THEIR LOCK!
THE "GREAT MAN," WHO KNOWS ALL ABOUT ANIMALS, EVEN ONES HE'S NEVER SEEN BEFORE!
IF ALAN HADN'T STOPPED THEM, THEY'D HAVE EATEN US BY NOW, AND THERE'S FOUR MORE LOOSE ON THIS PLANE!
HOW MANY MEN HAVE YOU GOT TO HUNT THEM DOWN?
BE QUIET!
NO WAY I WILL! YOU'LL HAVE TO SPRAY ME AGAIN, OR--
--OR--
HERE! THE ONLY OTHER MAN ON BOARD'S THE PILOT, SO IT'S UP TO US THREE TO DEAL WITH THEM!
HELPING YOU IS THE LAST THING I'D DO-- UNDER ANY OTHER CIRCUM-STANCES!
BUT THESE ARE THE ONES WE HAVE, DOCTOR!

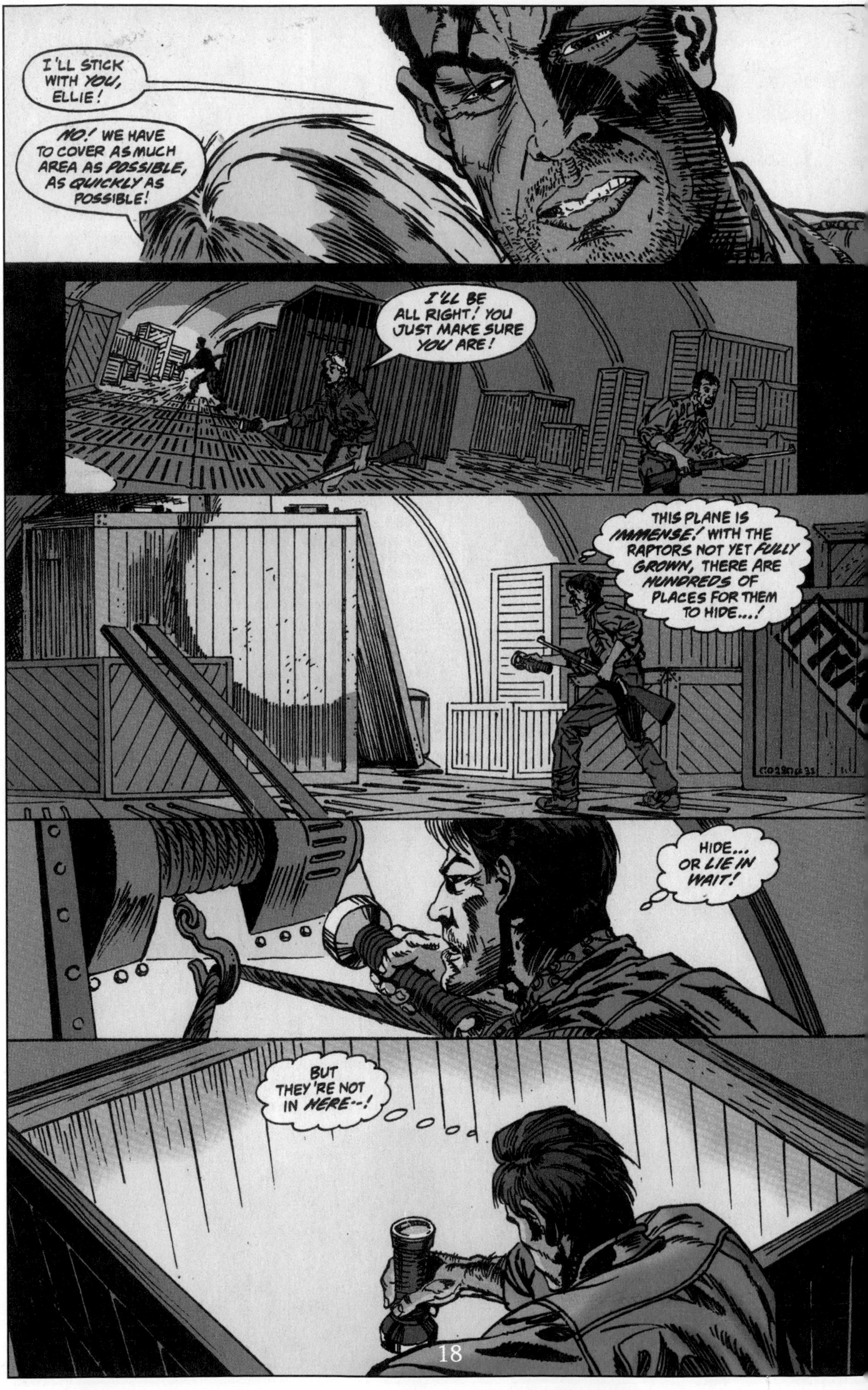
I'LL STICK WITH YOU, ELLIE!
NO! WE HAVE TO COVER AS MUCH AREA AS POSSIBLE, AS QUICKLY AS POSSIBLE!
I'LL BE ALL RIGHT! YOU JUST MAKE SURE YOU ARE!
THIS PLANE IS IMMENSE! WITH THE RAPTORS NOT YET FULLY GROWN, THERE ARE HUNDREDS OF PLACES FOR THEM TO HIDE...!
HIDE... OR LIE IN WAIT!
BUT THEY'RE NOT IN HERE--!

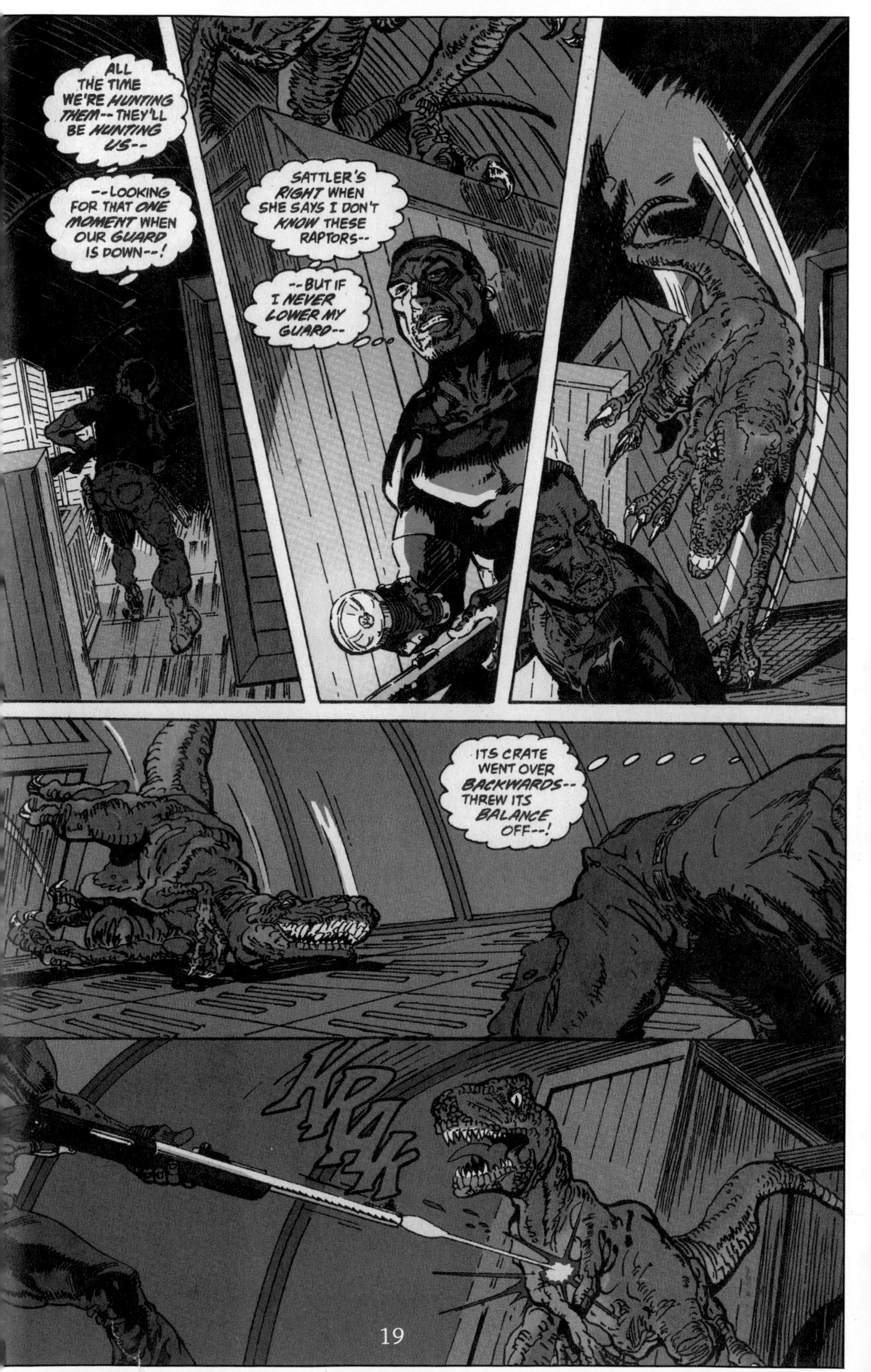
ALL THE TIME WE'RE HUNTING THEM-- THEY'LL BE HUNTING US--
--LOOKING FOR THAT ONE MOMENT WHEN OUR GUARD IS DOWN--!
SATTLER'S RIGHT WHEN SHE SAYS I DON'T KNOW THESE RAPTORS--
--BUT IF I NEVER LOWER MY GUARD--
ITS CRATE WENT OVER BACKWARDS-- THREW ITS BALANCE OFF--!
KRAKK

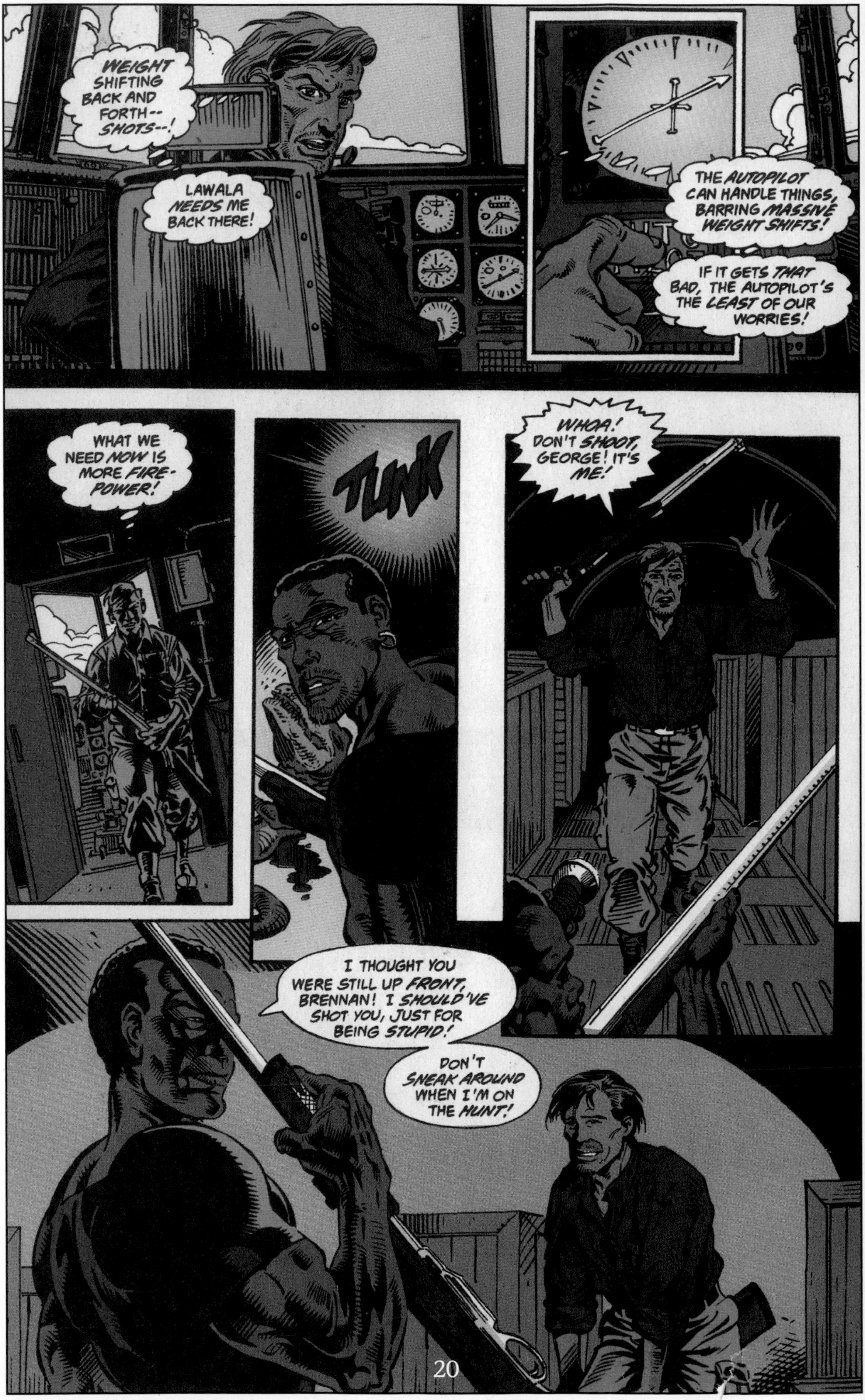

WEIGHT SHIFTING BACK AND FORTH-- SHOTS--!
LAWALA NEEDS ME BACK THERE!
THE AUTOPILOT CAN HANDLE THINGS, BARRING MASSIVE WEIGHT SHIFTS!
IF IT GETS THAT BAD, THE AUTOPILOT'S THE LEAST OF OUR WORRIES!
WHAT WE NEED NOW IS MORE FIRE-POWER!
TUNK
WHOA! DON'T SHOOT, GEORGE! IT'S ME!
I THOUGHT YOU WERE STILL UP FRONT, BRENNAN! I SHOULD'VE SHOT YOU, JUST FOR BEING STUPID!
DON'T SNEAK AROUND WHEN I'M ON THE HUNT!

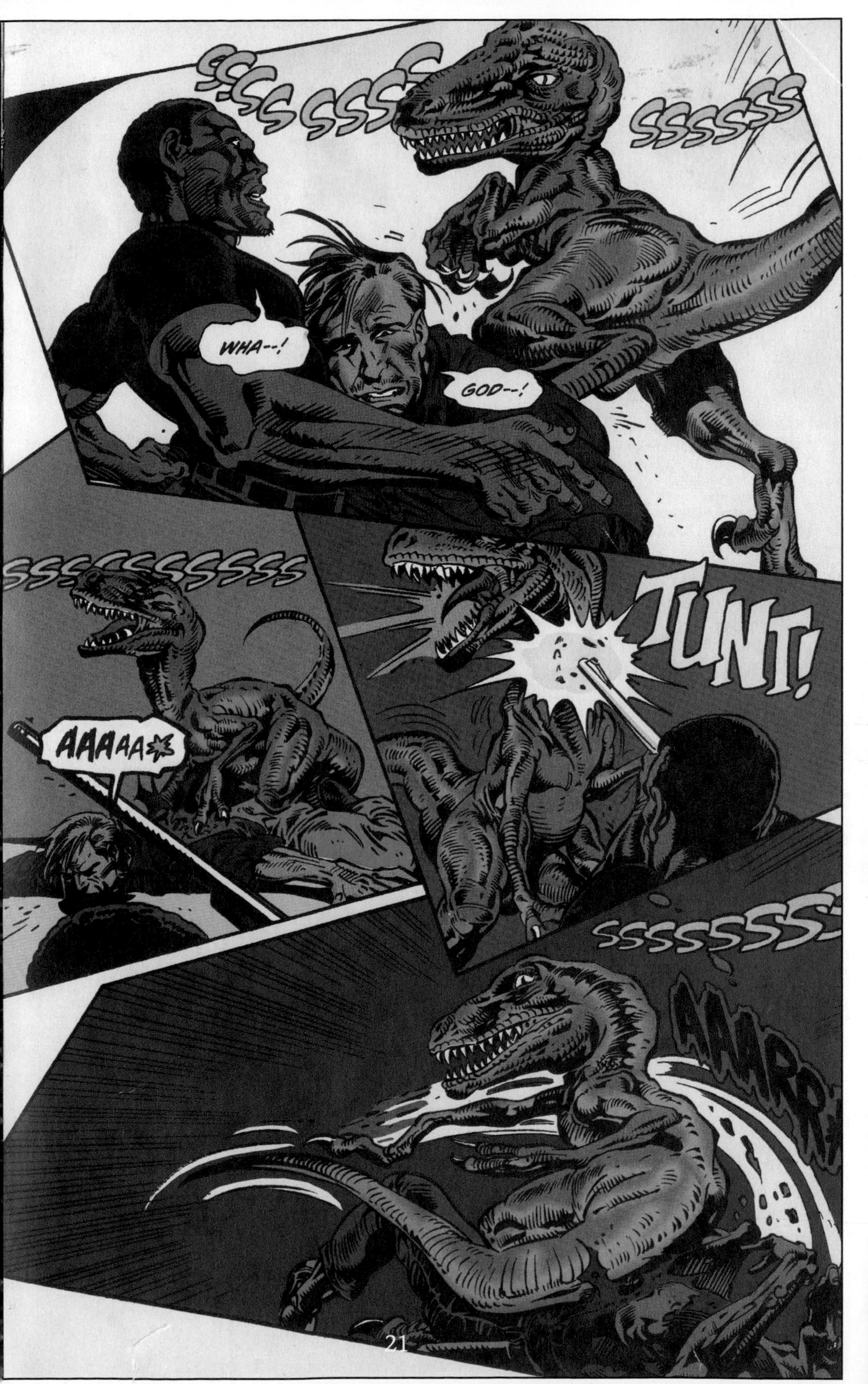
SSSSSSSSS
SSSSSS
WHA--!
GOD--!
SSSSSSSSSSSS
TUNT!
AAAAA
SSSSSSSSS
AAARR

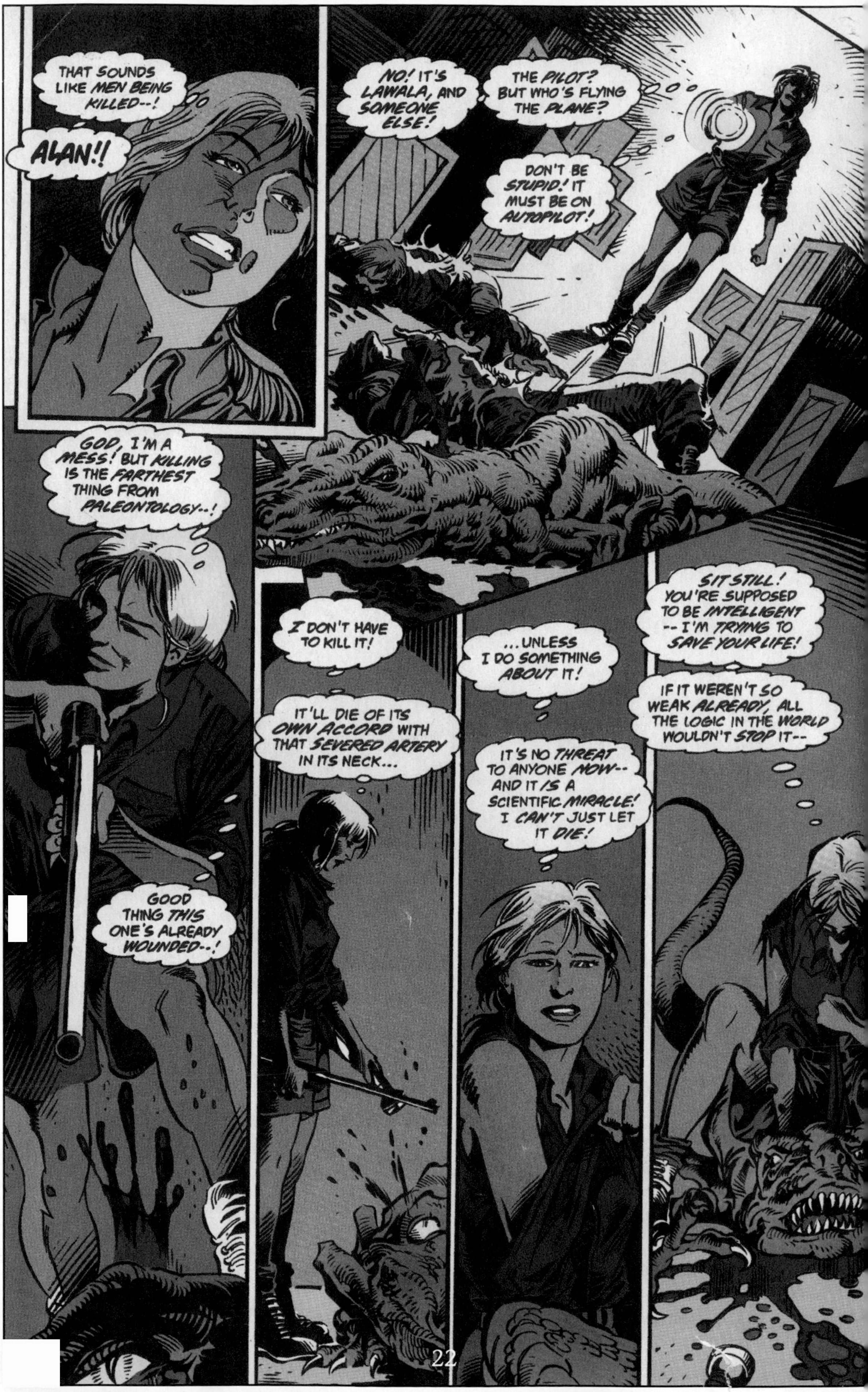
THAT SOUNDS LIKE MEN BEING KILLED--!
ALAN!!
NO! IT'S LAWALA, AND SOMEONE ELSE!
THE PILOT? BUT WHO'S FLYING THE PLANE?
DON'T BE STUPID! IT MUST BE ON AUTOPILOT!
GOD, I'M A MESS! BUT KILLING IS THE FARTHEST THING FROM PALEONTOLOGY--!
GOOD THING THIS ONE'S ALREADY WOUNDED--!
I DON'T HAVE TO KILL IT!
IT'LL DIE OF ITS OWN ACCORD WITH THAT SEVERED ARTERY IN ITS NECK...
...UNLESS I DO SOMETHING ABOUT IT!
IT'S NO THREAT TO ANYONE NOW-- AND IT IS A SCIENTIFIC MIRACLE! I CAN'T JUST LET IT DIE!
SIT STILL! YOU'RE SUPPOSED TO BE INTELLIGENT -- I'M TRYING TO SAVE YOUR LIFE!
IF IT WEREN'T SO WEAK ALREADY, ALL THE LOGIC IN THE WORLD WOULDN'T STOP IT--

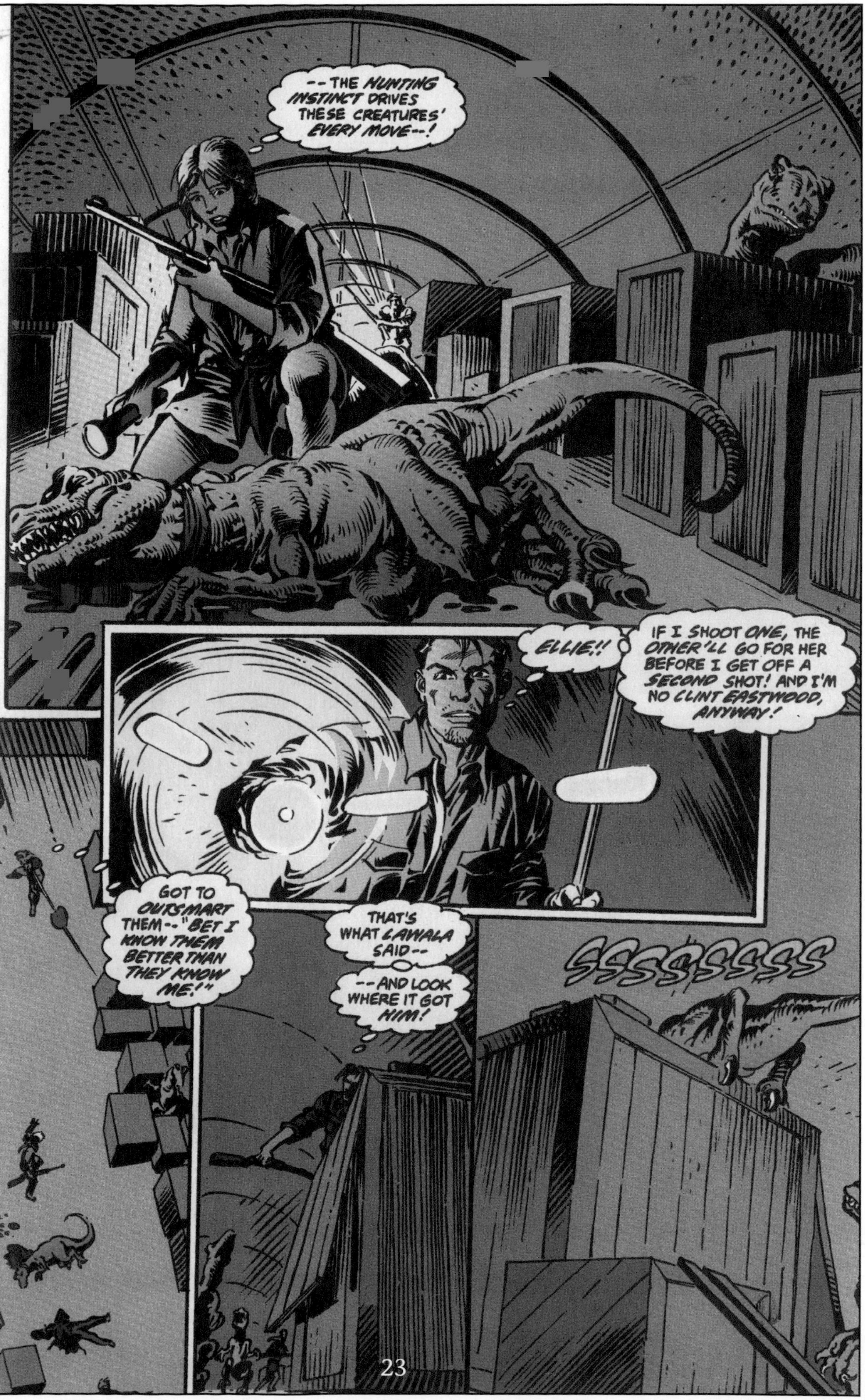
--THE HUNTING INSTINCT DRIVES THESE CREATURES' EVERY MOVE--!
ELLIE!!
IF I SHOOT ONE, THE OTHER'LL GO FOR HER BEFORE I GET OFF A SECOND SHOT! AND I'M NO CLINT EASTWOOD, ANYWAY!
GOT TO OUTSMART THEM--"BET I KNOW THEM BETTER THAN THEY KNOW ME!"
THAT'S WHAT LAWALA SAID--
--AND LOOK WHERE IT GOT HIM!
SSSSSSSSS

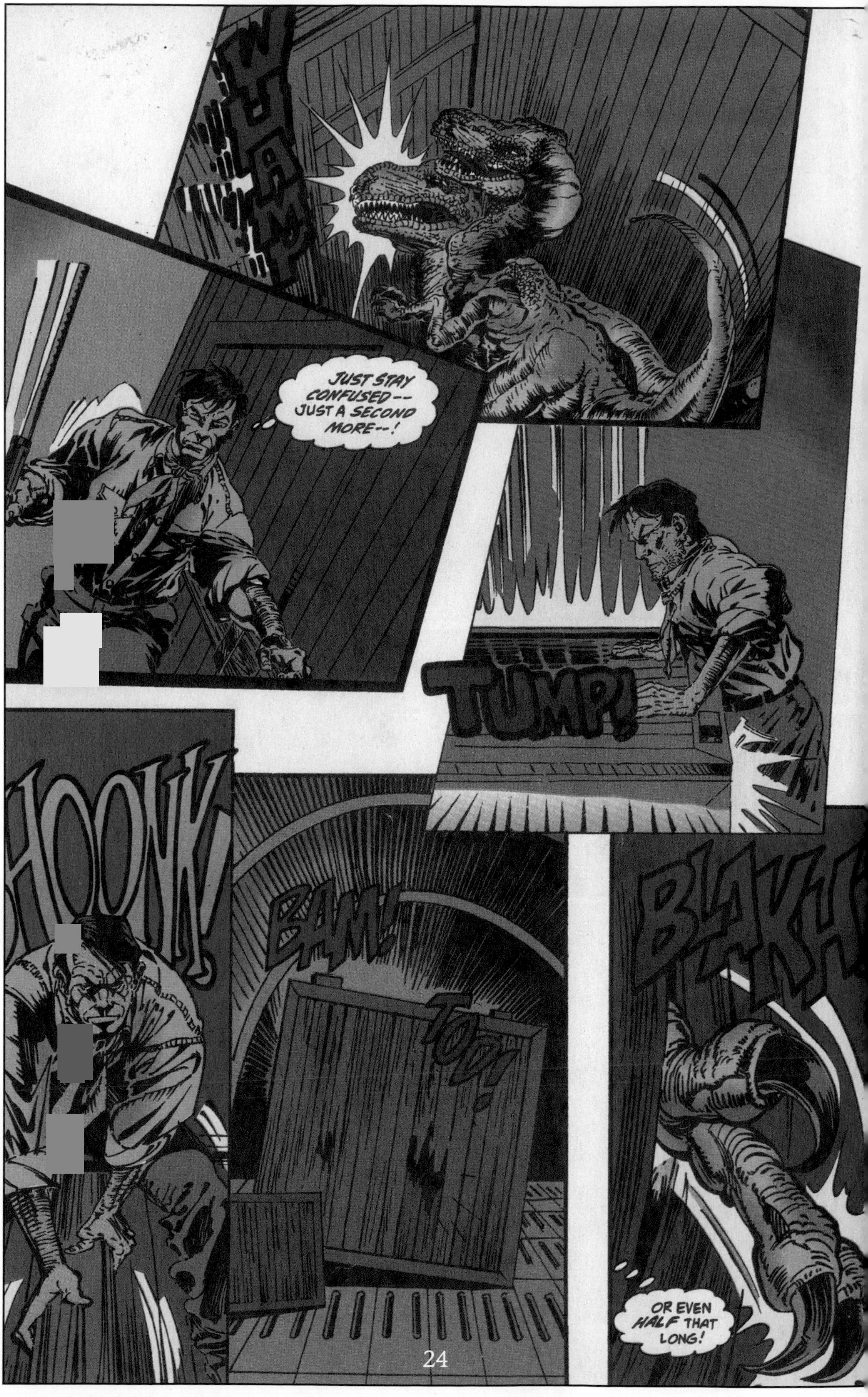
JUST STAY CONFUSED-- JUST A SECOND MORE--!
TUMP!
BAM!
OR EVEN HALF THAT LONG!

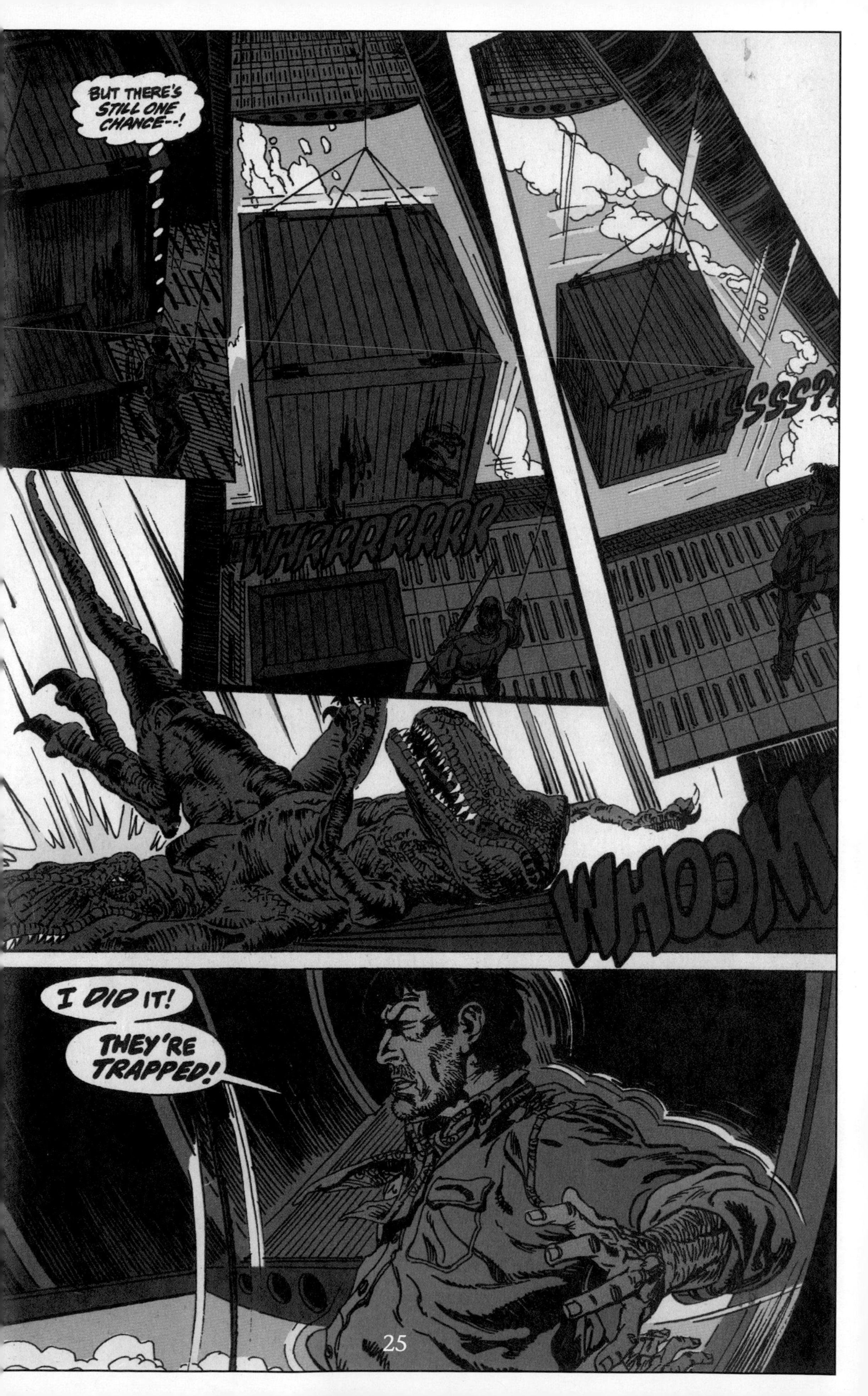
BUT THERE'S STILL ONE CHANCE--!
I DID IT!
THEY'RE TRAPPED!

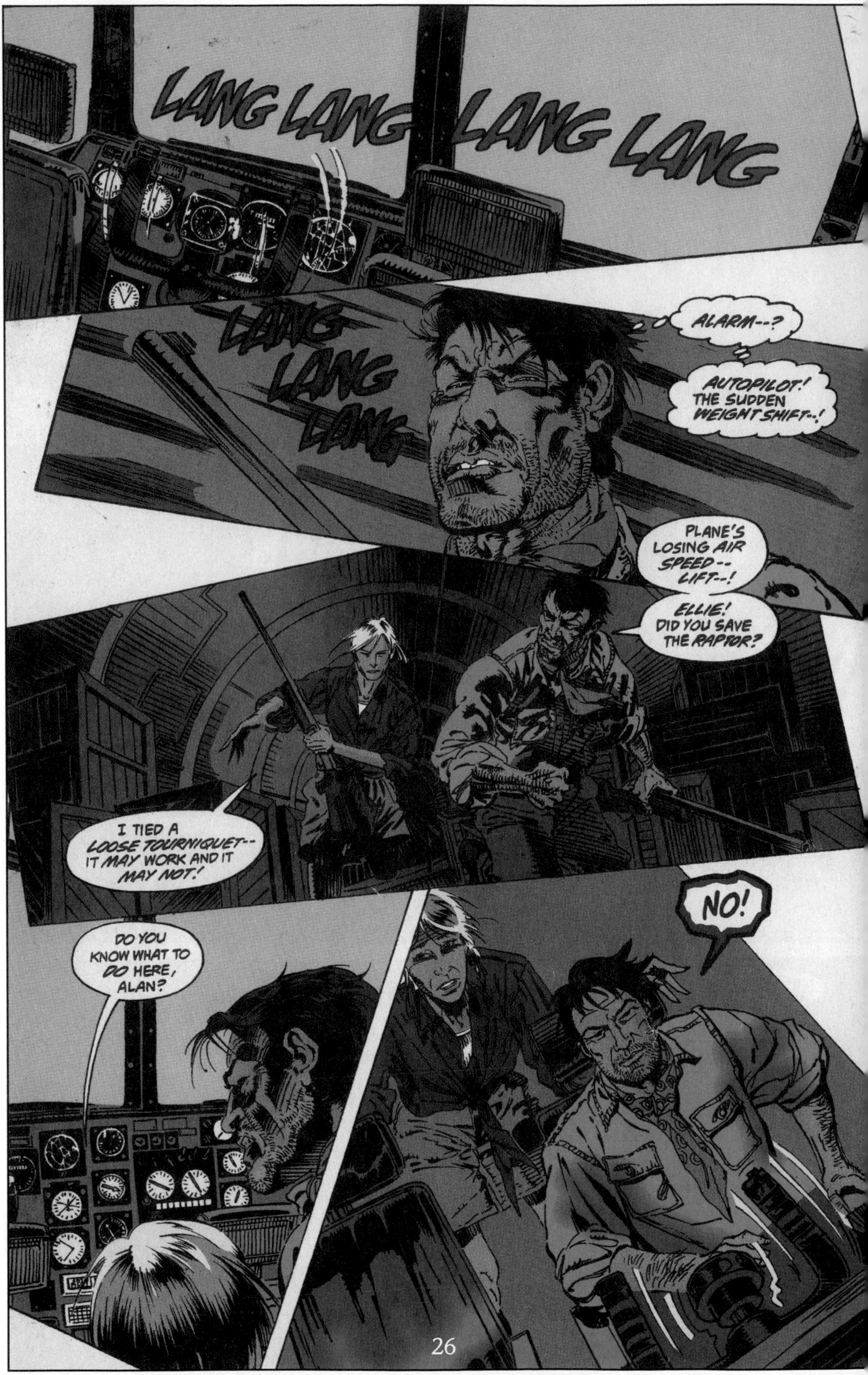
LANG LANG LANG LANG
LANG LANG LANG
ALARM--?
AUTOPILOT! THE SUDDEN WEIGHT SHIFT--!
PLANE'S LOSING AIR SPEED-- LIFT--!
ELLIE! DID YOU SAVE THE RAPTOR?
I TIED A LOOSE TOURNIQUET-- IT MAY WORK AND IT MAY NOT!
DO YOU KNOW WHAT TO DO HERE, ALAN?
NO!

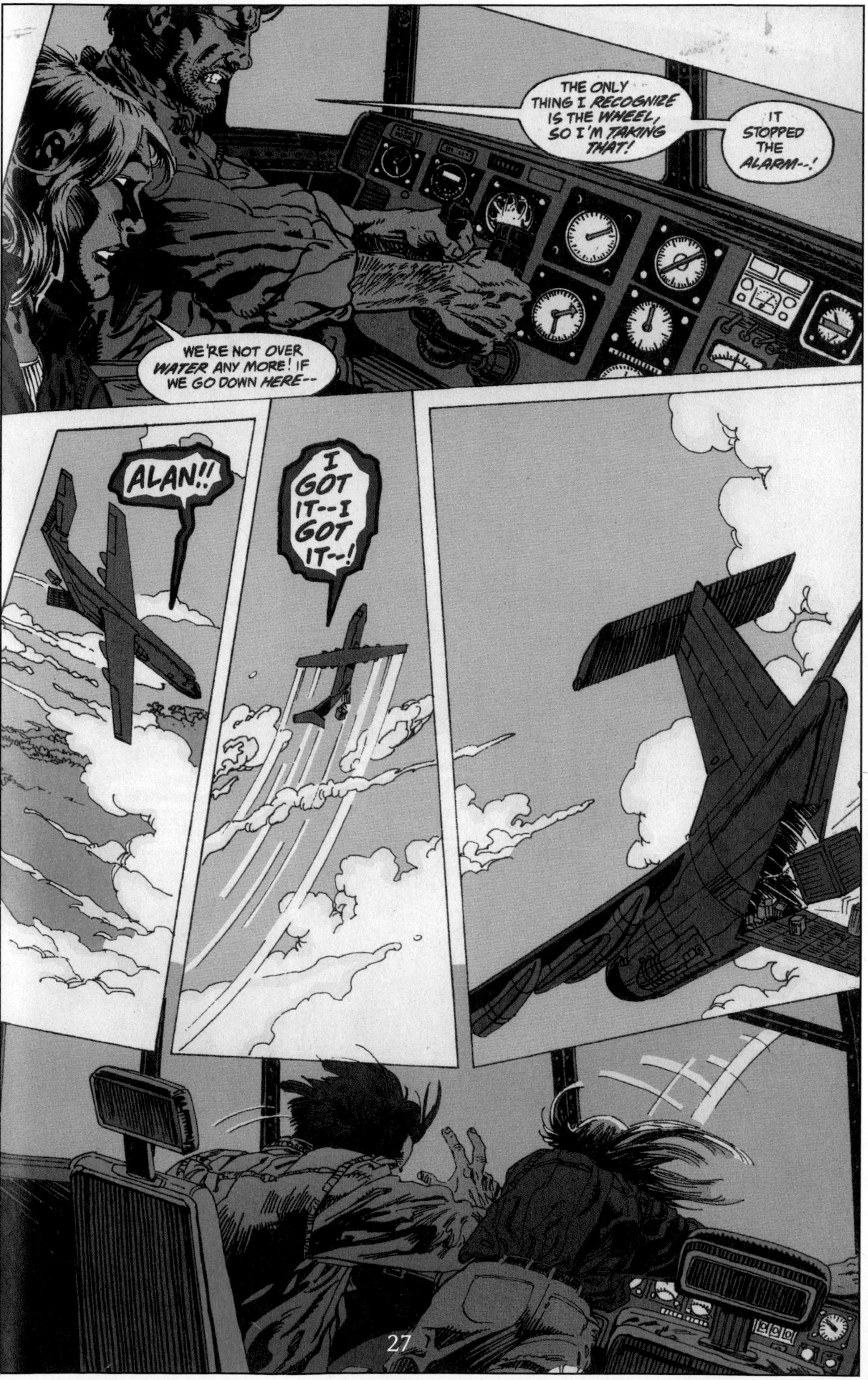

THE ONLY THING I RECOGNIZE IS THE WHEEL, SO I'M TAKING THAT!
IT STOPPED THE ALARM--!
WE'RE NOT OVER WATER ANY MORE! IF WE GO DOWN HERE--
ALAN!!
I GOT IT--I GOT IT--!

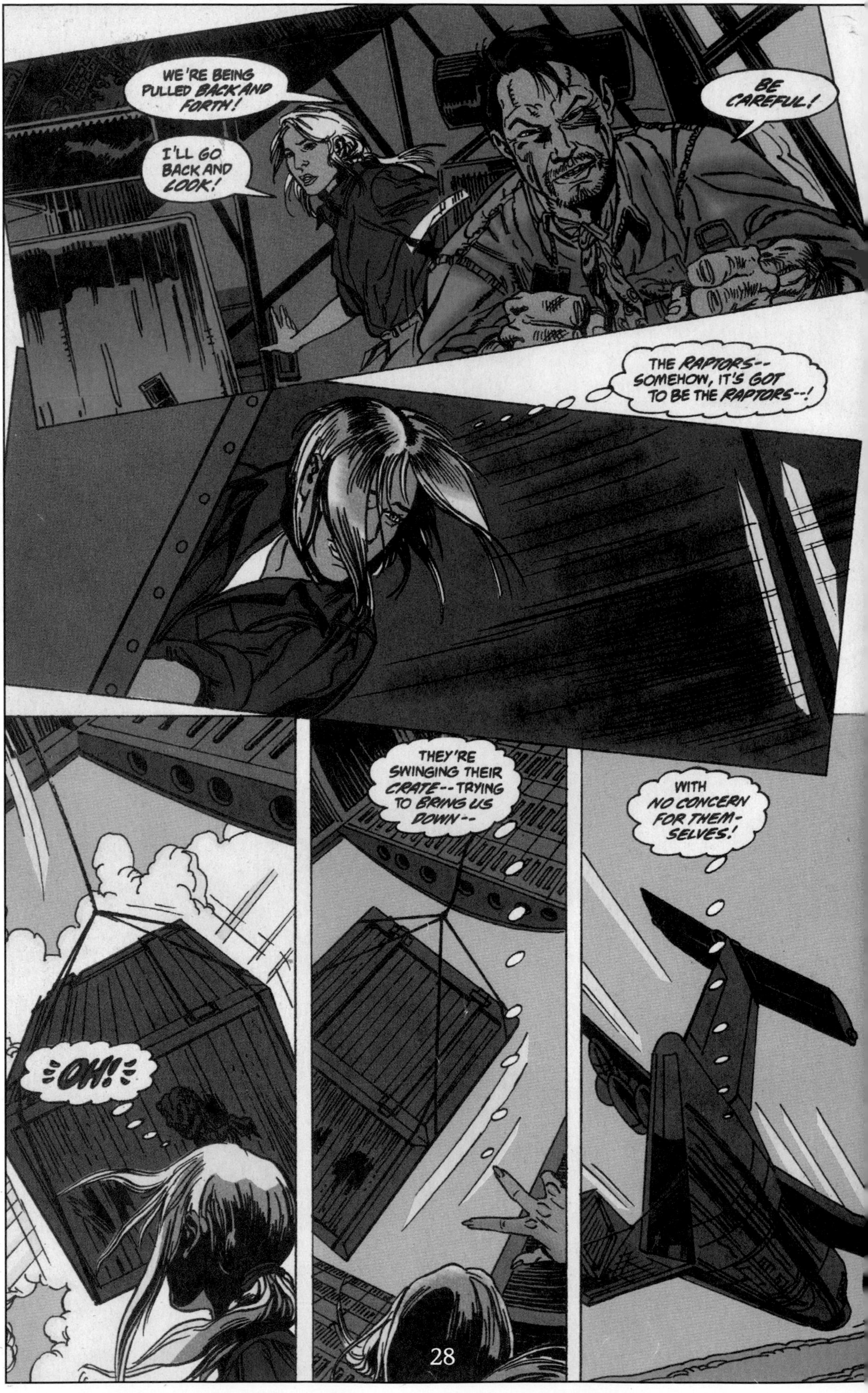
WE'RE BEING PULLED BACK AND FORTH!
I'LL GO BACK AND LOOK!
BE CAREFUL!
THE RAPTORS-- SOMEHOW, IT'S GOT TO BE THE RAPTORS--!
OH!
THEY'RE SWINGING THEIR CRATE--TRYING TO BRING US DOWN--
WITH NO CONCERN FOR THEM-SELVES!

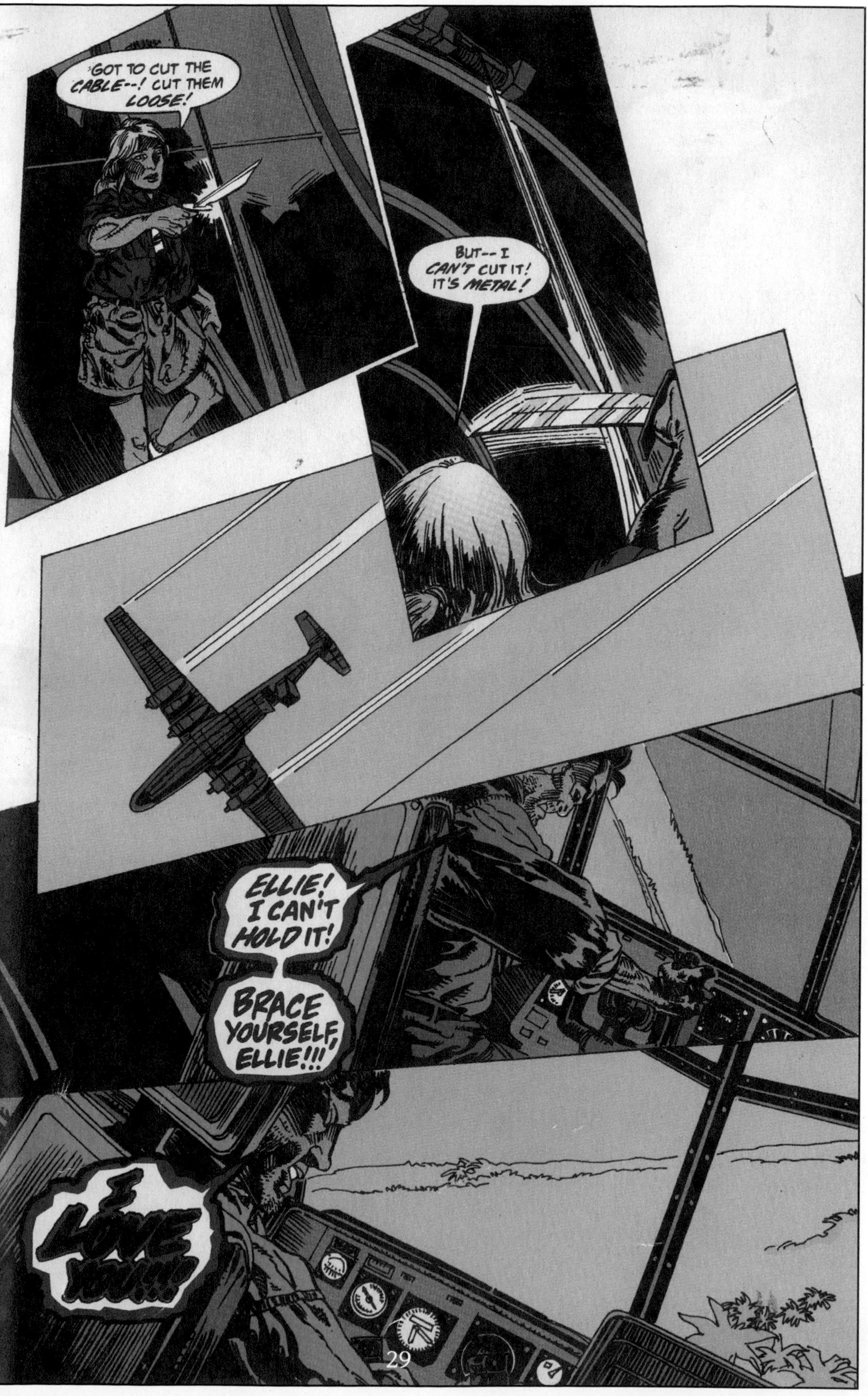
'GOT TO CUT THE CABLE--! CUT THEM LOOSE!
BUT-- I CAN'T CUT IT! IT'S METAL!
ELLIE! I CAN'T HOLD IT!
BRACE YOURSELF, ELLIE!!!
I LOVE YOU!!!

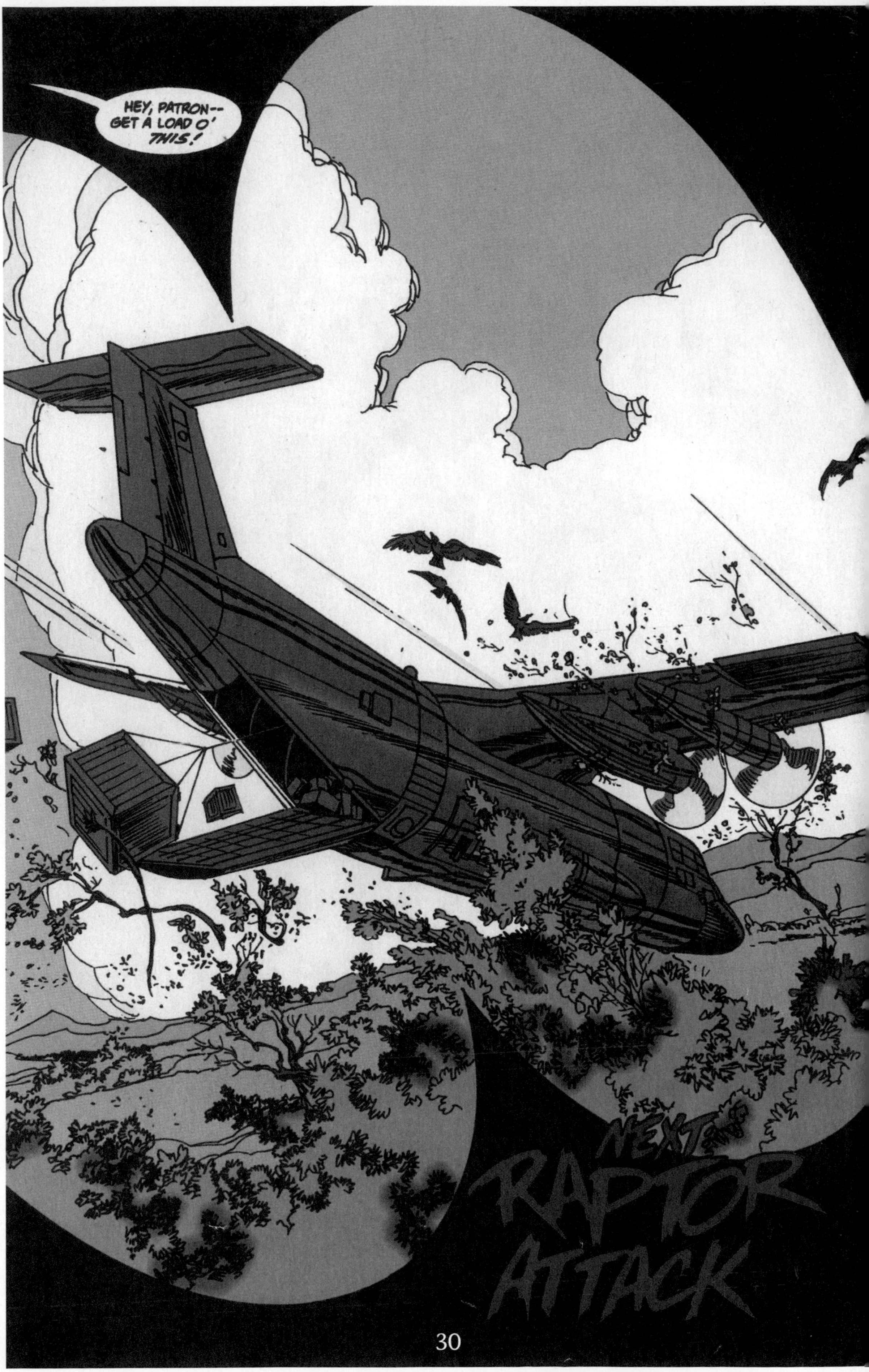
HEY, PATRON--
GET A LOAD O'
THIS!
NEXT
RAPTOR ATTACK